Last One Out

Last One Out

Jim Crigler

A Mason & Penfield Mystery

Book 4

Cover design by Rey Ortiz deadidlemedia@gmail.com

ISBN 979-8-9992595-3-0

Contents

Acknowledgement & Dedication

To Jennie: Your refusal to let me quit got me over the finish line.

Preface

Thanks for choosing the fourth Mason & Penfield mystery. I hope you find it satisfying.

The wheels of justice are said to turn slowly. I beg your indulgence if in these pages they seem to revolve at an unreasonable speed.

Saturday, October 20

7:00 p.m.

"Really, sir, do you presume?"

Tapers to either side illumined their table; sconces surrounding the room provided more ambient lighting; a nocturne by Balakirev wafted through the room from the piano in the corner on a hint of cinnamon; bone china with platinum rims awaited the first course. Water and wine stood in crystal between the candles; droplets adorned the water goblets like randomly scattered pearls in moonlight. The combined effect achieved the thoroughgoing elegance only possible through restraint.

The couple's dress was similarly understated: The man in a dark, bespoke English suit; the woman in a fitted caftan of dark navy linen with even darker embroidery. Her hair, lightened a bit from her natural brown, hung in a heavy braid, parallel to the slit opening of her frock, where her womanhood whispered. She smiled, at once demure and inviting.

"Why, yes," the man said. "Yes, I do. I do presume."

"And what reason can you give for your presumption?"

The groom, Ron Penfield, answered. "The cause of my presumption is the wedding we attended this afternoon."

Mirth lit Clarissa's eyes and the corners of her mouth as she asked, "And just who got married?"

His smile was full as he leaned forward and whispered, "I believe it was you and me."

Her eyes opened wide in mock surprise. "To each *other*?"

"I'm afraid so." Ron smiled that smile, the one broadcast happiness deeper than just happiness, beckoning his new wife to join.

Clarissa's smile now trended toward wonder, her eyes glistening to mute the light of the candles, and her breath caught. She couldn't speak for half a minute.

When her breath returned, she asked, "So in a greasy spoon like this, how does one order?"

"In this hash house," Ron replied, "one does not order. One merely eats the slop provided. Except when they serve chum."

Both broke out in laughter, taking the effort to subdue it for their surroundings.

And in due course, Mr and Mrs Penfield found that entrusting themselves to the chef's selection was well compensated. They similarly entrusted themselves to the sommelier with similar reward.

The *maître d'hôtel* attended their table after the first of three courses to be assured that everything was satisfactory; the chef similarly approached just before dessert. Both received their warrant. Chef and headwaiter wondered that the couple heard them ask.

When all was completed the Penfields strolled the quarter

mile to their hotel through a clear Atlanta evening that was cool, but not chilly.

The next day, they boarded a plane for Saint Marie.

7:00 p.m.

Lilia Argyros could never quite decide how to broach a new subject with her daughter.

Adena could be ... insistent on having her way. The focus her high-functioning autism brought to her every action made her seem to some to be completely unreasonable, but Lilia knew that Adena's focus was what made her test near genius in math and near prodigy on piano. At school, Adena was sometimes mocked — her classmates heard only her flat voice and saw only her limp hair and the way she dressed in nice clothes, but didn't seem to care.

Lilia slid a glass half of water toward Adena, who was working on a calculus problem. This was their signal that meant *When you can take a break, I need to talk to you.* Interruptions had in the past sometimes caused Adena to shut down entirely.

A minute passed as Adena continued working, her pencil scritching on her paper.

Two minutes.

Lilia waited, looking at her daughter but not staring, aware of, but ignoring, the white kitchen cabinets, the glass cooktop, the dishwasher still awaiting the dishes piled in the sink.

Almost three minutes, and Adena drew a small square at the end of the proof and set her pencil down. She stared at her spot, a knot in the oak of the table surface.

"Yes, Mother?"

Lilia inhaled and said, "Tomorrow, you will go to spend the day with your father."

Adena nodded. "Yes, we first talked about this ten days ago, and then again six days ago, and then two days ago. Each time was about an hour earlier in the day than the previous time, and now it is the night before, two hours later than the first time."

"Yes, dear. I want to make sure you understand, and you are prepared." Lilia had been in the U.S. since immigrating for college and staying. But as much as her accent had mellowed in seventeen years since she came from Athens — *the other Athens*, she told Georgians — she still seldom used contractions.

"What time should I be ready?"

"It is about a twenty-five-minute drive to your father's house, and we should be there by seven-thirty, so we need to leave at seven."

"I won't be going to church with you."

"No, dear. Is that a problem?"

Adena's gaze didn't vary as she — as Lilia knew she would — planned her morning to the minute. When that was complete, Adena glanced to the right and then back to her spot on the table and asked a question Lilia had sometimes pondered.

"Does Daddy really want to see me?"

Lilia understood the question. Lilia and John, just out of college, had been happy when they learned Lilia was pregnant, and their baby girl was beautiful, perfect in every way. But when Adena was diagnosed as autistic, John buried himself in his work, severely neglecting mother and daughter. Lilia had found comfort in other arms, then still others. When the third promised to leave his wife, Lilia filed for divorce, requesting full custody of their daughter. Then her paramour had not left his wife, had not married Lilia, had not adopted Adena.

So mother and daughter continued on their own.

For so long, John had continued to ignore them. For the little credit it was worth, he unfailingly paid child support and alimony, even when he acquired a new wife, even when he lost his job, even when he had become a lowly police trainee eight years ago.

A few months ago, Lilia had called Ann, John's present wife. John called Lilia back and invited them to an Independence Day cookout — a big gathering of friends and coworkers — and they had attended and reacquainted themselves with people from John's old, now defunct, employer. John had taken to Adena at once and showed her his roses.

And John had continued to see Adena every couple of weeks; sometimes Lilia stayed with them for the afternoon or the day, sometimes not. Lilia knew herself to be somewhat hotheaded (speaking conservatively), so she only stayed when Ann would also be there. The presence of others helped Lilia keep her cool. John had told Lilia that tomorrow, Ann would not be home due to the nature of her real estate business, so Lilia would go on to church.

And she knew that she needed to answer her daughter's — *their* daughter's — question.

"Yes, Adena. This visit was his idea. He asked if you could stay the whole day, and I was happy it worked out."

Adena's chin dropped a quarter inch and returned.

Then she began working on the next proof.

7:00 p.m.

Marlene Sauer would vent her spleen when people would pronounce her name "Mar-leen." Knowing Americans' propensity for phonetic spelling, and how the syllables worked out in their version of English, she would exaggerate her German accent when she corrected them: "Mar-LAY-nah. Like the actress, Marlene Dietrich."

When her husband, a lawyer, had resumed hard drinking after their toddler died of cancer, she had left him, divorced him, and moved to Atlanta, where she made a living for herself as a registered nurse.

Walter, her lover, had only mispronounced her name twice since she started seeing him. The second time was on a date, and her fury had uncharacteristically cowed him. After that he *never* got it wrong. She almost refused to go out with him again, but he had sufficient charm and black hair and a square jaw that made her think of Superman. Marlene knew Walter was married, but since he didn't seem to care, neither did she.

And now he was at her door with a pair of suitcases and a backpack.

Walter's wife had thrown him out. And Marlene let him in.

They ordered takeout tacos from the Korean fusion restaurant and drank Obolon Lager.

Opening second bottles, they settled on her worn, blue leather sofa. This was the only piece of furniture that seemed out of place; all the rest was upper-level IKEA-type Euro-modern. Walter guessed there was a story about the couch, but also decided that it was the wrong time to ask.

"So the Greek goddess tired of your seeing me, no?"

"Greek ... No. No. No, that wasn't my wife. She wasn't like my wife at all. She was just ..."

"... just someone you were seeing, the way you are seeing me."

He nodded, seeming insecure.

She thought, *He wonders whether* I *will show him to the door as well.* But she said, "If your wife is not tall and voluptuous with darkish hair, what does she look like?"

"Patty? Short, petite, short blond hair, trim, athletic."

"Athletic? What does she play? Tennis?"

"No," he said, "she competes in adult gymnastics — various events."

"Is she attractive?"

Walter nodded. "But enough about her. Let's talk about you and me."

"Very well. *Farbe bekennen.*"

He looked at her questioning.

"Show your colors ... um ... Put your cards on the table."

He inhaled slowly, apparently seeking the right words.

"Very well." He paused a few seconds more. "I need a place to live. I can afford to pay. I'd like it to be with you."

"Your cards are on the table indeed. But this is very brief — very sudden. What do you want for the long term? How do I know you will never leave *me* for someone younger and prettier and a better lover?"

Walter looked relieved. "Never is a long time."

"And it is a promise you made to your wife, presumably. You did not mean it then, why should I believe you mean it now?"

The look in his eye, the twitching of his lip, the shallow

breathing: He was a cornered animal looking for a way out. Not out of the apartment. If he wanted that, the door was only a few feet away, and he easily could afford a hotel.

His look softened, and he looked even more relieved. He looked relaxed.

"I did mean it then," he said. "And I do mean it now. Patty turned shrewish —"

"What is 'shrewish'?" Marlene interrupted.

"Shakespeare?"

Marlene thought for a moment. "*The Taming Of The Shrew*," she said. "A woman who nags and pesters and wants a life independent. Well."

She waited to see whether Walter would begin to squirm. He appeared to wait patiently.

"You may stay," she finally said. "Be warned though: I am ... what is the word? ... I am a stickler for neatness and cleanliness. These are habits that serve me well at work, and they serve me well at home."

Walter drew a deep breath and sighed. "I suppose I should go unpack. Or is there room in the closet for my things? You have two bedrooms — should I unpack in the spare room?"

Marlene's eyes opened wide and coy as she smiled and said, "Eventually."

Monday, November 5

7:55 a.m.

Ed considered the front of the Booker Medical Building as he sat in his car waiting for the offices to open. According to the signage, three different practices were listed, all loosely attached to the same hospital company, but with separate staffs. There was also a lab facility.

Ed was here to see his ex-wife, who, he had been told, worked here.

He looked at his watch. Four and a half minutes till eight o'clock. Thirty-five whole seconds had passed since the last time he looked. An older Accord pulled through the parking lot and circled around back. *I guess that's where the staff parks,* he thought.

Four minutes and three seconds.

He stared at the building. It was apparently only one story tall, though a second story might have been intended as an expansion at one time. Across the front, sections of brick and bare concete alternated, with windows in the concrete sections.

The front door was wide and apparently slid open automatically; when it was open, Ed could see an identical interior door.

A minute later, a tall, olive-complexioned woman came back around the corner from the staff lot and entered the building through the front door. He stared after her and forgot to look at his watch.

Three minutes even.

His heart was not racing, exactly, but he heard the pounding in his ears.

Ed's eyes lost focus, and he wished — no, he *didn't* wish for a drink. That was why he was here, because he had wished for a drink far too often and far too long.

Ed's hand drifted toward the car key settled in the ignition. He grasped it, deciding whether to remove it from its home or turn it and make the six-hour trip back to his home.

He sat like that, holding the key in place. What if she refused to see him? What if she called security or the police to have him ejected? What if she keeled over when he said what he had come for?

He knew all that was irrational. All except, perhaps, her potential refusal to see him. And he rated that less than half likely.

One minutes and five seconds.

Ed almost lost his nerve. Almost started his car. Almost drove away. Almost went back to Amory to lie to his group that his ex-wife was dead. To go back to his law practice as if he had just taken a long weekend, one planned when it had looked like the Braves might have a World Series slot. But not this year.

Eight o'clock.

A breath.

Another breath.

Remove the key. Pull the door lever and push open the door.

The sun just peeked over the hill and through mostly bare trees.

Ed entered the building. The slightly acrid smell of disinfectants greeted him under the fluorescent lights and the suspended, acoustical-tiled ceiling. There was a large waiting area that seemed to be shared among all the practices and the lab, with rows of chairs aligned in front of each reception desk.

Not knowing which practice Marlene worked in, Ed approached the first one he came to, the endocrinology group.

A pretty redhead, bundled up for an Arctic winter not yet arrived, greeted him in a twangy, very Southern voice.

"Do you have an appointment?"

He spotted her nametag: *Alice.*

"No, Alice," Ed replied, "I'm not here to see a doctor. I came to see a nurse who works in one of the practices. Marlene Sauer."

"You must know her, darlin' if you know how to pronounce her name."

"We've met." A humorless grin flickered across his mouth and disappeared. "Does she work in this practice?"

"No, not here. But you must be her new fiancé, Walter."

"No, I'm definitely not that. Which practice does she work in?"

"She works for the orthopedic group." Alice pointed across the way to another receptionist.

"Okay, thanks."

At the orthopedic reception desk, Ed asked the receptionist, a husky blonde named Ruby, for Marlene, and received the same remark about knowing how to pronounce her name, and the same question about being her fiancé. He disappointed his second receptionist, who asked him to have a seat.

While he waited, Ed dropped his keys in his jacket pocket and realized for the first time that he had been gripping them hard enough to leave impressions in his palm and across his fingers. He removed his cell phone from his pocket and looked at it for a second and held the power button until it started powering down.

When he looked up, Marlene was standing there, looking ready to spew acid on him. Despite her expression, her voice was neutral and quiet and professional.

"What do you *want*, Ed?"

Her hospital scrubs were oversized, but he could tell she had kept her figure. *Best not to think on that too long.*

His reply was as quiet as her question.

"I know you probably don't have time now, but is there a chance we can talk later? I . . . I have to . . . I need to talk with you."

"How long will this take?"

"Ten minutes, maybe fifteen."

"We had two cancellations in a row this morning. Follow me."

Marlene held the door for him, then walked around him while he waited for her. She led him through winding, beige corridors to an exam room and closed the door.

"Sit," she commanded.

Ed's choices were a molded plastic chair with metal legs, an exam table covered with white paper, and a stool. He took the chair.

"So now," she said, standing in front of him, hands clasped

behind her, "what is it you want?"

"First," Ed said, taking a breath, "I've been told by a couple of people you are engaged. Congratulations."

Marlene nodded acknowledgement but said nothing, just waited, expression unchanged.

Ed's heart resumed pounding in his ears. He counted ten beats.

"I'm here to apologize for hurting you. When Cory ... Instead of being there for you, I crawled into the arms of the bottle, and I stayed there and stayed there. And you did the only rational thing and walked away. The grief and despair — *your* grief and despair — were too much to bear on your own. I can never make that up; *nothing* could make that up." Ed drew a deep breath. "Will you ... *can* you ... forgive me?"

As she stared into his eyes, the hard set of her mouth held fast, but her own eyes softened a little.

Ed could see her jaw begin to open, her lips begin to loosen.

But she was interrupted by the clanging of an alarm bell.

"Fire alarm," she said. "Get out, if the front door is not blocked go out and at least half the way through the parking lot."

"But —" he started, and she interrupted.

"Go now! I must see to the clearing of our part of the building. We can talk later."

Ed exited the exam room, Marlene behind. She closed the door and hung a red tag that said *CHECKED* on the knob, then headed toward the back of the practice to begin clearing exam rooms, storage rooms, restrooms, and all the other enclosed spaces in the practice.

Ed took a wrong turn in the labyrinth of exam rooms and bumped into Marlene again.

"I told you to *go outside*!" she shouted. "Follow the signs you ..." She didn't finish the sentence, and she didn't need to — Ed had seen an exit sign for the first time, and he was already on his way to the lobby. After losing his way again and reorienting himself via the signage, he entered the waiting area.

No one was left in the waiting area by the time Ed got there. As he crossed, a short, blond-haired woman came out of the GP practice ahead of him. Catching a whiff of smoke, he picked up his pace. After he passed the door the short woman had come out of, he heard it open behind him and glanced back to see the tall woman he had seen before, who followed him as they all exited the building.

Ed's own car was about halfway through the parking lot, so he stood by it to wait as Marlene had instructed. He expected the alarm to stop any second now, but it kept on going. He still needed to arrange to talk to Marlene when he could peel her away from her duties and, perhaps, her fiancé.

The tall woman and three other people were standing by a balding man wearing a windbreaker over a shirt and tie and holding a clipboard. A fire engine and a fire rescue truck blazed into the parking lot, sirens adding to the alarm bell and the agitation of the people gathered there.

Hoses were being pulled from the engine, and two paramedics in smoke masks entered the building.

A couple of minutes later, the one of the paramedics returned to the parking lot, mask off.

Ed could see the man with the clipboard seemed agitated and spoke with the paramedic, who reentered the building, the alarm still sounding.

Most of the people in the parking lot had remembered to

bring their jackets, but not quite all. Those without jackets held their arms close to their sides and rubbed their hands together. A few of the men offered coats and jackets against the November morning to the women who lacked them. One of the women refused and appeared insulted at the offer.

One of the paramedics ran back out to the fire fighter who was in charge of the engine.

Suddenly, an announcement came from the loudspeaker on the engine: "May I have your attention please! Your attention please!" The alarm suddenly ceased, to everyone's relief. Relief was short-lived however, when the announcement continued. "No one is to leave the premises without permission of Dr ..." The microphone was still switched in but held away from the person holding it. "What name again?" Something indistinguishable was said. Then, full volume, "No one is to leave the premises without permission of Dr Workman. He will be at the parking lot exit along with someone to enforce this order. I repeat: *No one* is to leave this location without a confirmed medical emergency."

Ed was just starting to wonder what it was all about when two police cruisers pulled in, one to the front door, and one blocking the exit.

Ed inhaled sharply when he realized he had not seen Marlene in the parking lot. He hadn't seen her since she shouted at him in the hall.

Marlene was still in the building. And the police weren't allowing anyone to leave. Reflexively, Ed took a couple of steps toward the building entrance.

The man with the clipboard was trying to hold people back from the building. One officer from the police cruiser by the parking exit stayed there with the doctor, turning back people who wanted to leave; the other came to the door to hold people out of the building. From the other car, both officers entered the building.

Held up at the back of the crowd, Ed knew he wouldn't get any closer.

As he looked around, he saw the patrol car at the exit move, not to let anyone out, but to let in a two-door Infinity. The car parked alone as far away from all other cars as it could. A medium-tall, broad-shouldered man with a mustache, wearing khakis and a lined windbreaker came out the driver's door; from the passenger door, a tall woman of solid build, sun-bleached, brown hair in a ponytail to her shoulder blades, wearing a dark, heavy coat and dark pants.

8:32 a.m.

Detective John Mason and newly-minted detective Catherine Caligari circled the crowd in opposite directions.

"Stay by the door," Mason said when they met up in front, "and help the officer keeping people out."

Caligari nodded and introduced herself to the uniform.

Mason saw her take her badge from her pocket and hold it up so the crowd could see it. When a large man in shirtsleeves tried to barge past her to get to the door, she got directly in his way, so close he couldn't turn to go around her.

"Out of my way, little girl."

Mason winced as he entered the building. No one talked to Cal that way. Not twice, anyway.

Just inside the outer door, Mason put crime scene booties over his shoes. "Crime scene protocol in the waiting area until the forensics folks have cleared it," he said to the officers at the door. "Do you have any evidence markers?" he asked, referring to the little numbered "tents."

"No, sir," one officer said.

"Okay," he said to one. "Paine, go get some booties and come back. And while you're out there, get the fire fighters who entered the building to come and wait inside by the door."

Paine nodded and went to comply.

Mason waited by the entrance until the officer returned and donned the shoe coverings. He took a peppermint from his pocket and offered one to the officer, who declined. Despite the peppermint, which he made himself to get them strong enough, he could smell a whiff of smoke. So there was some evidence the fire alarm had not been irrational or faked.

They went past the rows of chairs to a practice entrance, where a muscular paramedic waited; her name tag said *Conlan*. She led Mason through the maze of hallways to where the other paramedic, a burly man named Grinvalski, waited beside the body.

"Tell me," Mason said.

Grinvalski said, "We came in, she was convulsing. We made sure her airway was clear, and we got a faint heartbeat."

"Then she stopped," Conlan said.

"People die unexpectedly all the time," Mason said. "Why did you call us?"

"Because there's a needle mark in her neck," Grinvalski said, pointing to the left side of the victim's neck.

Mason knelt beside her. "Looks like they got an artery." He stuck his tongue into his cheek for a few seconds.

"Okay, don't move," he said standing. "I'll get someone from CSU to clear you as soon as I can, then the medical examiner's folks will want to talk to you, then I will, then probably one other officer. Redundant and annoying. Either of you ever been at a murder scene?"

Both shook their heads *no*.

"It's a real pain." He looked at the uniformed officer. "No offence."

"Used to it," Paine said flatly.

Mason worked his way back to the waiting/reception area and to the entrance.

8:37 a.m.

Ed listened to the murmuring, sort of a subdued hubbub, from the people around him.

Five minutes later, the mustached man came back out and called in a loud voice, "Can everyone hear me? No?" He got the microphone for the loudspeaker from the cruiser. "I am detective John Mason. There has been a suspicious death in the building. Marleen Sauer —"

Someone interrupted to shout *Mar-LAY-nah*.

"Thanks," the detective said. "Marlene Sauer is dead under suspicious circumstances. As soon as we can, we will let everyone inside to get out of the cold. We will need to get names and addresses, and to talk with everyone here. In the meantime, please *do not* talk with each other about anything you may have observed this morning. We need everyone's *independent* story about the morning. Again, please wait patiently, and please do not compare notes. Thank you."

Ed found himself unable to breathe for a moment.

8:40 a.m.

Lanny Johnson was leading the CSU team, and Mason gave him instructions: Clear the area the body was found in and talk to the paramedics; clear the waiting area and a couple of restrooms near the waiting area, in that order. Mason and Caligari would find where the fire was started.

Mason put on fresh booties and called Caligari to go with him. As they were searching for the room where the fire had occurred, an odd question came to Mason.

"Cal."

"Sir?"

"I told you about that. It's 'John' or 'Detective,' depending on who's around. Now: Did anyone ever call you 'Cath?' "

Caligari sniffed. "Yes, when I was in middle and high school. But when I got to college and there was a nursing school, it suddenly sounded too ... hygienic? clinical? medical, anyway. So I changed the nickname to Cal, and no one has objected. Not event dieticians."

Mason laughed out loud at that.

After a several minutes, they found the source of the fire in the lab area: A three-foot-high bright silver trash can. It wasn't airtight, but it had a gap almost a quarter inch wide around the rotating lid.

"Whadaya think?" Mason asked.

"First, it stinks, like cloth was burned. Next, it's confined. Next, assuming cloth was the fuel, it wasn't stuffed full, and it seems to have burned itself out."

"Good. Anything else?"

"Most ... of ... the ... time —" Cal looked at Mason. "Detective, are we ready for working theories yet?"

"Sure, I'll take a preliminary. What?"

"Most of the time," she said slowly, "trash cans are kept near a wall. This is in the middle of an exam room. Not near anything else that might burn. The lid would make air exchange slow."

Mason was impressed. "Conclusion?"

"The fire was set by one person who then skedaddled. The idea was to get someone else to pull the alarm to clear the building while the murder took place. Given the vic was killed in the orthopedic office, the perpetrator — the person who set the fire — had time to get there, assault the victim — how was she killed?"

"She has a needle mark on her neck, with bruising around it."

"So the victim was assaulted while the building ..."

"... was being cleared." Mason finished. "What we have here is first-degree murder. If the coroner brings any different conclusion ..."

"... it will be our fault," Cal finished, "for not presenting the case correctly."

"Yep."

After a few seconds, Mason added, "I hear people entering the building, so the waiting area is cleared. Let's go organize the interviews."

8:57 a.m.

Given the large number of people, Caligari and three of the four uniformed officers would be interviewing people. With everyone inside and restrooms almost ready, Mason gave instructions to the officers who would conduct the interviews.

1. Name, address, phone, occupation
2. Physical description of the interviewee
3. Reason for being in the building, e.g., medical, staff, patient, whatever
4. Where were you when the alarm sounded?
5. Who was near you when the alarm sounded?
6. Did you know the deceased, Marlene Sauer? If so, what was your relationship?
7. Did you see or hear anything unusual?
8. Did you take any pictures or video at the building today?

Anyone saying anything "interesting" or "unusual" was to be sent to Mason, Do Not Pass Go, etc. Also, receptionists, head nurses, office managers — anyone who had authority in some vague sense, needed to talk to him.

The fourth uniformed officer was stationed at the door with instructions not to let anyone out of the building without a signal from one of the interviewers.

Another squad car arrived. Mason sent one of the officers to get the license tag numbers from all the cars; the other was to check for any recorded video of the scene.

As he was dispatching the last pair of officers, Mason noticed Lilia Argyros, his ex-wife. She sat perfectly composed, perfectly at ease, not talking with anyone.

Caligari was just finishing with an interview and sending

the subject out when Mason caught her eye. She walked over.

"Last summer at the picnic, did you meet my ex-wife?"

"I was wondering whether you noticed she's here," Cal said. "I think we said hello, not much more."

"Interview her next. Let her go unless she has something relevant. I already know she's an office manager, so she's exempt from that bit."

Cal nodded and went off to do as requested.

An officer, named Briggs, who had been sent to look for video came back empty handed. "There's a camera outside and one here in the waiting area," he said, "and there may be more through the building. But I can't get into the security office."

"Find the on-site building manager," Mason said. "If he won't cooperate, if he even hesitates, bring him to me and interrupt whatever I'm doing. In fact, even if he does cooperate, I need to talk to him."

One of the officers brought Mason the woman who activated the fire alarm, blue dye still covering her left hand. She was a nurse, with *ELOISE* printed on her nametag. She chafed at having to go through it all again.

"Why did you pull the alarm?"

"*As I told the officer*, I pulled the alarm because I smelled smoke. I knew it wasn't tobacco or anything else people smoke on purpose, so I assumed there was a fire. *Was* there a fire?"

"Someone set a very localized fire that stank and produced a lot of smoke," Mason said. "Once the building has been cleaned and aired out, no one will know there was a fire. What was going on at the time?"

"Our practice had just finished the morning staff meeting. I was on my way to find the list of appointments, smelled smoke, pulled the alarm. Then I left the building right away."

"I suppose you have annual fire drills."

She nodded. "The last one was just a couple of weeks ago. All the procedures were fresh in everyone's mind."

"So tell me about the procedures. I suppose everything is standardized for the building."

"Exactly." Eloise was relaxing now that she wasn't repeating answers she had already given. "Medical staff see to helping patients exit. One of the staff clears the unoccupied exam rooms, storage, restrooms, whatever. When a room has been cleared, we hang a red tag on the knob, so no one has to spend time checking that room again."

Mason nodded. He had guessed as much from his previous visits to his own doctor: Tags hung inside each door would be moved to the outside as rooms were verified to be empty.

"So did you see or hear anything unusual this morning?"

Eloise shook her head no.

"How well did you know the victim?"

"Just to say hello."

Mason thanked her and told her she could leave. But then . . .

"Wait a minute."

Eloise turned around.

Mason said, "There must have been some kind of roll call protocol, to know that everyone was out of the building."

Eloise nodded. "Each practice and the lab has a 'door checker' like I described, and also someone to do roll call outside, including patients and everyone. The checkers then go to the building manager or someone he designates."

A pretty standard way to handle things, Mason thought. "Okay, thanks."

He looked around the room and saw that Cal was no longer talking with Lilia, so she must not have known anything relevant. Lilia wasn't in the room either, so she must have left.

While Mason was thinking how he was relieved not to be talking with his ex, Officer Paine approached, accompanied by a man wearing a shirt and tie and windbreaker and holding a clipboard.

"Detective, this is Mr Stotts, the building manager. I have his particulars."

Mason thanked Paine, who went to find someone else to interview. He saw Briggs walking through the waiting area and motioned him to come over.

"Mr Stotts, this is Officer Briggs. I need you to turn over any site video you have from, say, six a.m. on."

"I'd need some kind of authorization to turn that over."

"This is a murder investigation. Please help us with our investigation."

"HIPPA law —"

"— doesn't apply," Mason interrupted. "We aren't asking for anything medical or confidential. We just want video of public areas, places anyone standing around would see — the parking lot, entry, waiting area, hallways if you have them. That kind of thing."

"All right. I'll have a copy made."

"Thanks. Before you go to get it, can you describe the emergency procedures the people here follow."

Stotts went through the procedures the nurse had outlined, with a few more details. Each practice was to muster and have its roll checked outside; roll checkers then reported to Stotts. The checker for the orthopedic group had accounted for everyone: medical and support staff, patients, everyone but

Nurse Sauer. She would have been expected as one of the last people out the door because her duty in an evacuation was to verify all the rooms in the practice had been vacated. When the fire fighters and paramedics were informed that she still wasn't out, they reentered the building and eventually found her body.

"One last thing," Mason said, "I need the names of the people assigned as room checkers in the various parts of the building."

Stotts looked at his clipboard. "That's easy: Marlene Sauer in the orthopedic group; Lilia Argyros, the office manager for the general practice group; Karla Landon, an office assistant in the endocrinology group; and Sophie Brent in the lab."

"Can you think of anything else I need to know?"

"It probably doesn't matter, but Nurse Sauer had put in two weeks' notice at the beginning of last week. She just became engaged."

"Who was going to replace her — in her emergency duties, I mean."

"It would be up to the practice to designate someone."

Mason thanked Stotts again and sent him off to retrieve the video and turn it over to Briggs, who would give it to one of Johnson's CSU people.

An officer named Doss came over.

"Got something for me?" Mason asked.

"It seems there's someone here who didn't get logged by the staff. Not a patient — someone who came to see the victim. The receptionist — the bundled-up redhead over there, said a man asked for Marlene Sauer by name. She said he pronounced her name correctly."

"Is he still here?"

"Yes, Detective. I had her point him out. The guy in the middle of the room with the blue windbreaker, gold arrowhead logo on it."

"Bring him here right now."

"Can I let the receptionist go?"

"Get the man's movements in the lobby in order, then she can go. But find anyone he talked to and see if it all lines up."

The man who approached with Doss seemed familiar. Doss handed the man off to Mason, then left to finish interviewing the receptionist.

"I'm Detective Mason. Please sit down Mr —?"

"Penfield. Edward Penfield. Call me Ed." Ed paused for a couple of seconds. "Didn't I see you at Ron's wedding a couple of weeks ago?"

9:33 a.m.

"Yes, that was me," Mason said smiling. "I'd like to talk more later, but given the number of people we have to interview, I need to get right to the point."

"Sure."

"I'm told that you came here today asking for Marlene Sauer. Is this correct?"

"Yes."

"Why was that?"

"Marlene is my ex-wife. Or ... was, I guess."

Mason stared for a minute. "I see. And you were here to visit her. Have you been here to see her before?"

Ed shook his head. "No, never have." Ed blinked and a tear rolled down his cheek. "I haven't seen her outside of a courtroom for eight years." He wiped the tear away with the back of his hand.

"Until today."

"Until today. I came ... Look, Detective, the reason we divorced was my out-of-control drinking. I came to ... ask ..."

Mason waited, guessing he knew what Ed wanted to say. It was important for both of them for Ed to finish the sentence unaided.

"... to ask her to forgive me."

There it was. "How long have you been sober?"

"Six months and three days."

"Congratulations. Do you live in the Atlanta area?"

"No, I practice law in Amory, Mississippi. And thanks."

Mason nodded. "So you were in town two weeks ago, but you didn't come to see Marlene then."

"I intended to. But I didn't. I should have."

Ed's face twisted and his hands began to shake.

Mason gave Ed time. Which he took.

When he had calmed down, Ed said, "The stupid fire alarm," and more tears streamed.

When Ed had again regained control, Mason said, "You were interrupted by the fire alarm?" Ed nodded. "What then?"

"She commanded me to leave. I tried but got turned around and wound up meeting her in a back hallway. She pointed out the right way, and I went out to the parking lot."

"Was there anyone else back there? In the exam rooms or offices or hallways or anywhere like that?"

Ed thought a minute. "I don't think so. When I got out here to the waiting area, no one was here. A couple of people came out of one of the other doors and left at the same time I did. We were the last people out of the building. Or close to it."

Mason thought, *So he was the last person to see Marlene Sauer alive. Or close to it.* He hoped the 'close to it' was correct. But he had to find out for certain.

"How did you get into the back of the practice?"

"I asked for Marlene at the desk. The receptionist thought I was her new fiancé."

"That must have been uncomfortable."

"Just saying 'no' was easier than trying to explain."

"Sure. What then?"

"Marlene came out. She asked why I was here. I said I needed a few minutes to talk. She said they had cancellations and took me to an exam room in the back. We were just starting to talk when the alarm ..." Ed trailed off.

"And then you wandered around until you got to the waiting room and left the building."

Lips pressed together and face scrunched up, Ed nodded yes.

Mason handed him a business card. "Here's my info. If you think of anything, anything at all, I need you to call."

He turned and called "Detective Caligari!"

Cal put her interview on hold and came over.

"Yes, detective?"

"This is Ed Penfield." Her eyes widened slightly, but she didn't say anything. "Give him a business card. I've given him mine." He turned back to Ed. "As I was saying, if you think of anything at all, give me a call." As Cal handed Ed her card, Mason went on. "If I don't answer, you can leave a message, but call Detective Caligari. Make sure you actually *talk* to one of us."

"Will do. Is there anything else?"

"You're a lawyer, so you'll understand: Since you seem to have been the last person to see Ms Sauer alive, I need to have someone search you and your clothing. And, with your permission, your car. Also, I'm afraid I need you to stay in the area. You were here early, so I guess you had a hotel last night."

Ed nodded.

"Or maybe you can stay with Ron."

"I was going to talk to Ron while I'm in town, for the same reason as Marlene. He's back from his honeymoon, but I doubt I'll be able to stay with him. I'll check back into the hotel and try to handle clients from here."

"That would be a big help. Call and leave a message for one of us with your contact details."

Mason called a uniformed officer over to take Ed to an exam room and check his clothing and his person, and then to go with him to check his car.

5:09 p.m.

The only interviews besides Ed Penfield's that contributed anything were the two receptionists Ed had spoken with. Monday morning had been quiet. The receptionist for the orthopedic practice confirmed that the two earliest appointments had called late in the previous week to cancel, and no other patients had come to fill in.

The doctors had nothing to contribute, and neither did the

head nurses. The other receptionist, the one Ed had not talked to, had not even noticed him crossing the waiting area from one reception desk to another.

Mason made sure Mr Stotts, the building manager didn't leave. Stotts had nothing more to contribute, but he did have full access to the building. "And you can make sure we don't violate patient confidentiality, as well." That seemed to put him at ease, since it gave him an Official Duty.

Office staffs were allowed to go to work to reschedule appointments set for the day. Lab personnel were allowed to process whatever needed to be processed. The police presence would disrupt everything else, and bringing in people who were not there at the time of the crime would only add unhelpful confusion.

The Crime Scene Unit had a lot to do. Per Mason's instructions, they had already gone through the waiting area so everyone in the parking lot could come inside. Then while the area around the victim was being processed, one team member worked the two restrooms nearest the lobby: one in the lab section, one in the endocrinology practice.

The room where the trash can fire had been set was thoroughly examined, and, as Lanny Johnson, the CSU lead, said, the trash can itself was "taken into custody."

At the end of the day, Mason told Caligari, "Go home. Sleep. Be prepared for a sleepless couple of days. There's going to be a mountain of reports to go through. And we need to examine physical evidence as well."

Cal asked, "Is eight early enough in the morning?"

"Make it nine, I have a stop or two to make before we start. If you get to the station before I do, go ahead and start reading. You can draw conclusions if any seem obvious, but hold them loosely. There's something subtle going on here, and any theories we come up with are subject to correction."

6:02 p.m.

A couple of days home from their honeymoon, Ron and Clarissa Penfield sat in their kitchen. They were making eyes at each other across the corner of the table when the phone rang. It took Ron a minute to decide to answer.

"Ron, I think I'm in trouble."

Silence.

"Not again, Ed."

Ed had been in town, in the church, even, for Ron's wedding to Clarissa a couple of weeks before, but they hadn't spoken beyond *hi*, and that was more than they had said to each other in four years.

"No, no, no! It's not like that! I haven't been drinking."

"Right. Okay, so what is it?"

"Marlene is dead."

"That's too bad." Ron snapped. He paused a second, and then said more gently, "Really, I always liked her. I'm sorry to hear. So why are you in trouble?"

"The police think I may have done it."

"Where are you? Didn't I hear she moved to Birmingham?"

"No, I'm here. Atlanta."

Ron's eyebrows went up. "She was living here?

"Yeah. She was working at a doctor's office two miles from your house."

"Wait ... Have you talked with the detective?"

"He told me not to leave town." Ed was sounding more and more discouraged.

"What's his name?"

"You know him — he was at your wedding. Mason. John Mason."

Bristow. Very local. "Why does John think it might have been you?"

"Because I'm the last person to see her alive. Other than the killer."

"Why is it murder?"

"He didn't say. The only thing I heard besides *don't leave town* was *suspicious circumstances*."

Both paused for a minute.

Ed asked, "Look, is there any way we can meet? I was going to try to talk to you on this trip, as well."

"I ... don't think that's a good idea."

"I understand. If you change your mind, you've got my number."

"Yeah, I've got it."

"I'm going to be working out of my hotel room. I have clients who have litigation coming up. But I can meet daytime with an hour's notice. Faster in the evening or early morning."

"I'll remember that."

They rang off.

6:13 p.m.

Clarissa said, "Was that your brother?"

Ron nodded.

"Did I hear you say 'murder'?"

Ron nodded again.

"Who?"

"His ex-wife, Marlene. She had gone back to her maiden name, Sauer. She worked at a doctor's office somewhere around here. He was there when she was killed."

"That's awful. You mean he witnessed it?"

"Not quite. He was around. I think he came to town to talk with her."

"Did they have any children?"

"They had a son. He died of cancer when he was three."

"Dear God, that's worse!"

"He . . . *they* were hard partiers before little Cory was born. When he came along, they slowed down and were good parents. But when Cory died, Ed drank to forget. And when that didn't work, he drank some more. He never forgot Cory, but he *did* forget Marlene, even though she was still right there. She was smart enough to leave him. They were divorced, and I lost track of her."

"At the wedding, you said maybe three words to him."

"Probably less."

"He had to introduce himself to me — otherwise I wouldn't have known him from the mayor of Macon. What happened between you?"

Ron didn't answer.

"Ronald Charles Penfield. I'm your wife — I need to know these things."

After a minute Ron nodded. "You're right. Mom died a year or so before Cory. But Dad died after. By that time, Ed spent more time drunk than sober."

Clarissa didn't look like she believed him.

"Okay, that's probably exaggerating, but not by much. Anyhow, Ed *was* drunk at Dad's funeral. He had to have help to walk thirty yards to the graveside for the burial. After that, I decided I didn't need a brother. He didn't even *come* to Barb's funeral."

Ron's face hardened. "And that's the way that is."

Clarissa reached across the table to grasp Ron's hand. She hadn't seen him like this before.

Before Ron and Clarissa were both widowed, they were neighbors. Clarissa was divorced before her husband died, and Ron's wife, Barbara, had been a friend, almost Clarissa's only friend after her divorce. Barb had died a few months before Abe. A few months after that, Ron and Clarissa had gone out for dinner, and then they started seeing each other regularly. Clarissa went to church with Ron's family, where she was converted and baptized and catechized and more amazed every day at how forgiveness extended even to her.

There was a lot they still had to learn about each other, but Clarissa now knew what was hurting her husband. The scab over the emotional hurt was preventing it from healing.

My husband! Just thinking those words almost took her breath away. And she determined that she would find a way to help him heal.

That sat silent for several minutes.

"I'm sorry," Ron said.

"For what?"

"For ruining the moment, the mood."

Clarissa shook her head. "Moments and moods come and go."

The corner of Ron's mouth turned up wryly. "For newlyweds, it shouldn't happen that much."

She smiled her most enchanting smile. "Get your running shoes on. Let's get some air and clear our heads."

A couple of minutes later they were on a walk-and-run through the sunny, autumn-glorious afternoon.

Clarissa set a fast walking pace. Ron worked at keeping up. Before they started dating last summer, Clarissa had been overweight. But after recuperating from her appendectomy, she had started walking and eventually graduated to running. Her weight had dropped to reveal a lovely figure.

To prevent getting up to running speed, Ron said, "So we need to start moving the rest of your clothes and things across the street." He was only panting a little.

"Sure. I was going to ask Lenna to help."

"I could help and we could start this evening."

"Tell you what," Clarissa said, "we'll call you to do the heavy lifting. Now *run*!"

She took off ahead of him.

Tuesday, November 6

7:44 a.m.

"Thanks for meeting me before work." John Mason spoke with Lilia Argyros, the office manager for the General Practice group. She also happened to be his ex-wife.

"It is *very* early for you," Lilia said.

They sat in a fast-food dining room, John with coffee, Lilia with tea and a cup of fresh fruit. Her very professional suit couldn't obscure her mind-numbing beauty. John had maneuvered them to a corner as far as possible from the door so the inevitable stares wouldn't distract from their conversation.

"Is this about Adena or the death at work yesterday?"

"It's the latter, I'm afraid. I need as complete an account as you can give of everyone's movements from the time you arrived at the office until you left the building after the alarm."

"I thought so. I arrived a couple of minutes before eight, parked around back in the staff parking area."

"Are there reserved parking spaces?"

"Yes, but only the doctors have assigned spaces."

Mason nodded.

Lilia continued. "I went directly to our office, checked to make sure all the scheduled people were in, and went to my little coffee room."

"And made espresso?" John smiled with recollection. "In that mug Adena made when she was little?"

Lilia nodded, smiling gently. "Double espresso. It's as close as I can get to *proper* coffee outside my apartment and the Great Northwest. I checked office supplies, and I was about halfway through the espresso when the alarm sounded. It is my duty to check rooms and hang the tags on the doors, so everyone knows which rooms require no further checks. When I completed that, I left the building."

Mason looked at Lilia's hands. Still no rings.

"Okay, did you see anything unusual, see anyone who shouldn't have been there, overhear anything weird?"

"No one."

"And since you were making sure all the rooms had been checked, you were last out of the practice, right?"

"Yes. I heard a door, I think it was a restroom, and saw a shoe going around a corner, but the way the halls twist around I could not see who it was. She was hurrying faster than I was."

"Why 'she'?"

"It was just an impression. But it was a small shoe. Does that count?"

"Not as evidence, but it leans toward your being specific, and if it becomes important, it can be a starting place."

Mason took a breath.

"So when you got to the lobby — the waiting room, I mean — did you see anyone?"

"Yes. There was a man who was medium height, not much overweight."

"Could he be attached to the shoe you saw coming out of the restroom?"

"No, the shoes were wrong; he was wearing black dress shoes; the shoes I saw coming from the restroom were white trainers, like the kind nurses wear."

"And when you got outside?"

"I went directly to Mr Stotts to tell him that our practice had been cleared. He had a checklist. He has a checklist for everything." She smiled. "You are, I think, familiar with the concept."

Mason snorted lightly. "It keeps me from forgetting things."

Lilia looked at him and shook her head. *Old business*, she thought. *Not my problem anymore.*

8:48 a.m.

When Ron Penfield opened his front door, he looked at Mason and said, "I guess you're here about Ed."

Mason nodded.

Ron motioned him in, and they went through to the kitchen.

Ron and Mason didn't see, but as they entered the kitchen, Clarissa, coming down the back staircase, stopped near the bottom and scurried, lightfooted, back up. She wasn't dressed to see company.

"When I called, I was surprised you told me you were home."

Ron motioned for Mason to sit at the table and went for coffee mugs.

"Clarissa and I both have another week off work. Lenna and Ed — my Ed — are at school, Gloria is in Houston, and Ron — Ron Jr, I mean, has moved out to a house he's sharing with some college pals."

"Does anyone say 'pal' anymore?"

Ron poured two mugs of coffee and got a small carton of cream for Mason.

Mason stirred in his cream and said, "So tell me about your brother."

Ron inhaled and exhaled.

"Ed is a small-town lawyer in Mississippi. We grew up in another small town, Houston. I went technical at Ole Miss, he got a history degree at Mississippi State and went to law school in Clinton." Ron sipped his coffee. "He was always a hard drinker, starting in high school. He was also adept at test taking, so he always did well. He and Marlene met when he was in law school — she also partied pretty hard, I guess. They got married between Ed's second and third year. After law school, he took over the law practice in Amory. He sometimes gets clients from Tupelo who want a lawyer from out of town. And he continued country-club drinking, claiming it helped his law practice.

"But when Marlene became pregnant, they slowed down. Cory was born and they were good parents. Not perfect, but in some ways better than me. But when Cory got cancer, they were distressed, and when he died, Ed started drinking hard again. Marlene finally couldn't take it anymore and left him, and they got divorced.

"I just found out when I talked with Ed last night that she had moved here."

Mason nodded. Everything aligned with what he had learned from Ed the day before.

Clarissa appeared again at the foot of the back stairs, wearing jeans and a loose pullover shirt and deck shoes, her long braid over one shoulder, lips glossed and light makeup over her tanned cheeks. Most of all, she smiled, not just with her mouth, but with her whole face, her posture, her whole being.

"Hello, Detective!"

Ron stopped breathing for a minute at the sight of his wife.

"Hi," Mason said. "Please call me John. I guess it has been a couple of years since we got to say more than 'hello' and 'congratulations.' "

Ron poured half a mug of coffee for Clarissa and pointed to the cream in front of Mason.

Clarissa smiled and sat down. "Mm hm. Since you knocked on my door after ... after Barbara was killed."

They all became quiet for a moment, remembering.

"But now," Mason said, rescuing the mood, "you two are married to each other. As I said at your reception, I hope for all the happiness you can find."

Both smiled, and Clarissa's gaze dropped shyly. "Thanks," they said in unison, then turned to each other and laughed.

Clarissa finished filling her cup with cream and stirred.

Ron looked at Mason and pointed at Clarissa. "Tea drinker."

Mason nodded with good-humored understanding and said, "You know Ed is in a twelve-step program, right? AA, or similar?"

"He didn't say so, but I guessed as much."

"He told me yesterday that when he was in town for your

wedding," Ron reached and took Clarissa's hand, "he wanted to talk to Marlene, but didn't, and he probably wanted to talk to you then, too.

"From my perspective," Ron said, "it's better he didn't. We were busy." He winked at Clarissa.

Mason said, "It's none of my business —"

"— You're right," Ron interrupted. "It isn't."

Mason took the hint and said, "Look, since Ed's in town anyhow, you *may* wind up talking with him, no matter how estranged you are. If he does, and if he says anything that winds up being material to the case ..."

"... give you a call. You can count on it."

9:50 a.m.

Mason walked into the detective squad room at nine fifty. He saw Caligari at her desk, which faced his own, plowing through reports.

"How long have you been here?"

"Since eight thirty," Cal said, not looking up.

"Interviews?"

"Mostly. Glanced at the nothing in the forensics report."

"Coffee?" Mason asked.

"Had some, thanks. Water, if you have a minute."

"Sure," Mason said, taking Cal's glass to the bottled water dispenser.

When he set it down in front of her, she thanked him, folded her hands on her desk and closed her eyes for a moment. Then she drank off half the water and looked up. "I should have done that a while ago."

Mason indicated the stacks of papers in front of her. "So what have you learned so far?"

"Marlene Sauer was very particular about people pronouncing her name correctly. She was a good nurse, with bedside manner — do you say 'bedside manner' outside the hospital? — anyhow, she was better with patients than some, but not as good as others.

"With other members of the staff she could be ... exacting. Another nurse borrowed her jacket once — a generic, white, doctor's office jacket, nothing special — and Marlene reamed her out for it."

Cal consulted the running notes she had been taking.

"As we heard in interviews, she was recently engaged. Apparently, she either wasn't going to need to work or she found other employment, because she put in two weeks' notice about a week ago."

"Do we know who the fiancé was?"

"Yes. A patrol unit sent to her apartment found a man there named ..." She looked at her notes again. "Stancill. Walter Stancill. Haven't looked into him yet."

Cal looked up at Mason, suddenly worried.

"Wait ... one of ..." She shuffled some more of the papers and pulled one out. "It's not a common name. One of the interviewees was a Patricia Stancill, a nurse."

"Which practice did she work in?"

"She worked for the GP office."

Mason said, "So Patricia worked with my ex-wife. We can ask Lilia about that. And their office is on the opposite corner of the building from the orthopedic office where the victim worked and was found. Make a note, we need to confirm where Patricia Stancill was when the alarm sounded."

Cal wrote it down.

"Who had anything to say about Ed Penfield?" Mason asked.

"Only the two receptionists. Oh, since he wasn't a patient or staff, he wasn't on the roll call outside the building."

"So if he had played his cards right, he could have just walked."

"Your notes said he's a lawyer," Cal said. She drank half her remaining water and said, "so he should have known that. So if he's the killer doesn't that make him dumb?"

"Or smart for getting us to think it would be dumb."

Cal nodded and stared at her water. "How about Ms Argyros?" she asked.

"Lilia? I had coffee with her this morning. I had her confirm some details."

"She was the last person out of the building."

"She was last because she is the room checker and *had to be* last," Mason said. "And she works in the GP office, anyway."

Cal finished her water. "Which, as we already said, is all the way across the building from the orthopedic docs, same as that nurse, Stancill."

"Exactly."

"So she probably *couldn't* have seen anything."

Mason tapped a knuckle. "You said there wasn't anything in the forensics report. Just how much nothing was there?"

"There were no indications in the area around the body."

"Whoever it was wore clean shoes in a doctor's office. I'm shocked. What about the trash can — the one with the fire?"

"It was stuffed with a generic lab coat, a small amount of lighter fluid in it. Guaranteed to smoke and stink, and likely to go out after a few minutes in a can like that one."

"Find out whose coat it was. If there's no name tag or anything, we'll have to call everyone until we find out. M.E.'s report?"

"Haven't seen the preliminary yet."

Mason called the Medical Examiner's office and found out that the report had just been posted to the server.

The mark high on Marlene Sauer's neck was indeed the injection site for a toxin. The toxin was in the "aldehyde" family, the family that included formaldehyde, but it wasn't the body preservative used by morticians and bug collectors. The injection had been made with a 6-millimeter hypodermic needle; the syringe had bumped the neck hard enough to raise a light bruise. The needle pierced through the external carotid artery and stopped inside the internal carotid where it crossed back under the external. The toxin was delivered directly to the victim's brain.

"I don't get about arteries crossing," Cal said.

Mason explained. "The main carotid comes up from the heart and splits into an internal and an external; 'external' just means closer to the skin, not outside the body. When you take your own pulse on your neck, you are touching the artery before the split. The internal starts out going toward the center, but it crosses back under and heads more toward the front of the brain. It's like the I-75 interchange at the I-285 bypass on the north side: if you're southbound and want to go east, you exit right which puts you to the west of the westbound exit but then one ducks under the other.

"So they cross and go the right way."

Mason nodded but said nothing.

"Soooo ..." Cal said. "Lines of pursuit?"

Mason inhaled. "One: Finish reading the interview reports,

see if anything turns up. Two: Go through the video and see what order people left the building. Concentrate on the last dozen or so."

"Why so many?" Cal said as she typed. Everything was on the department computer; she was entering Mason's list into the shared whiteboard software. They could both see it and annotate it at the same time.

"Because if the killer came out of the building, it'll be one of them. And the ones who *aren't* the killer are also the most likely to have seen something. Three: victimology. Learn who she was. Four: Learn more about Walter Stancill. Five: Find out whether Walter's related to Patricia Stancill. Having the same last name is too much coincidence."

"How much *wouldn't* be too much?"

"Where they bought gas," Mason said. "Where they shopped for groceries if it's not too far away. Incidentals of life are not relevant unless too many of them pile up. Six: go through everything the CSU collected and photographed. And seven: Look into Edward Penfield."

Cal finished typing. "That's a lot to do."

"I told you not to expect much sleep for the next couple of days." Mason stood. "Let's go look at the physical evidence."

Both got up and moved toward the stairwell. They turned a corner.

Cal said, "About Edward Penfield ..."

"Yeah?"

"We picked out Stancill because of the last name. 'Penfield' isn't that common, either. Is he related to that guy who was at your picnic last July?"

"Very good. Yes, Ed and Ron are brothers."

"Is that going to be a problem?"

"No. I never met Ed before yesterday, and the brothers are estranged. Ron won't try to protect him."

They opened a door to the stairwell and began the descent. Cal spoke more loudly to make up for the echo all stairwells have.

"Do we know why they don't get along?"

"Ron wouldn't tell me specifically, but it's wrapped up in Ed's heavy drinking. You read my interview notes?"

Cal nodded, then realized that Mason couldn't tell what her response was since he was leading. "Yes. He's in a twelve-step program of some kind."

"And", Mason added, "he admits to being one of the last to leave the building."

They stopped in the stairwell in front of the door on the floor that Forensics was on.

"So, opportunity," Cal said. "Motive?"

"She's his ex-wife, so there was some acrimony there before yesterday. But he was there to apologize as part of his AA."

"He *asserts* that," Cal insisted. "We need verification."

"Right. We try to verify everything independently. Most of what we do is drudgery: Check this, verify that, ask him, interview her. We may uncover something else while we're working this case — not certainly, but certainly possible. What I said yesterday, about subtlety: Our first job is to eliminate the impossible."

"The Sherlock Holmes method."

Mason grasped the door handle and turned it. "Let's go see what's not impossible."

10:35 a.m.

Lanny Johnson was on his feet, headed away from the doorway, and thus the detectives, when they stepped in. He said "John" as he turned around, but before he could see them.

"How did you know it was us?" Cal asked.

"Detective Mason comes and goes via the stairs more than anyone else."

"And if it hadn't been us?"

"Then Knop's first name is John; I would walk over to him." He had pronounced his name *kuh-NOPP*, much to the tech's annoyance. "You're here for the Sauer inventory."

"Were there any grapes?" Mason deadpanned.

"That's the other reason," Lanny said. "I could feel the joke coming in the stairwell. But you didn't come here for badinage. Follow me to the box of wonders. And no Pandora jokes."

Mason snapped his fingers in mock disappointment.

As they made their way to the table, Lanny continued. "Being a medical office, it was pretty clean."

"One would hope," Cal muttered.

"That means, as you will see in the report, that there were no fingerprints that revealed anything. Every print we found was someone who worked in the same part of the building."

"How about the trash can?" Mason asked.

They turned the final corner and entered the evidence examination room.

"The trash can had zero prints or other residue. The recoverable parts of the liner had no prints. But it's a medical office."

"So lots of people wear gloves," Mason said.

"Including the janitorial staff," Cal continued.

"Exactly," Lanny said, fetching the first box from a shelf. "I know already that you will, but it's my job to be redundant and tell you to make sure stuff you get out of the boxes" — he was getting the second box — "goes back in the same box it came from."

"Welcome to the Department of Redundancy Department welcomes you," Mason got in before Lanny could stop him. "And yes, we will be careful of that."

Lanny pointed to a couple of larger boxes in the corner. "Those are the trash can itself and the ceiling tiles from the room you found it in. We had to get the building engineer to get the tiles, and *he* had to get new tiles from a warehouse, so we just got them ten minutes ago."

The CSU lead left the detectives to their work.

The first box included a floor plan of the entrance and the waiting area, with a grid overlaid, scaled so each cell represented a one-foot square. Each bag with a recovered item was annotated with number of the grid it had been found in. Most of it was minute scraps of paper or hairs. All the data and photos of the evidence would be on the server, but examining it in person would still have value.

The contents of the lobby trash cans were similarly sparse. They were of the same kind, silver metal cylinders with rotating lids in the dome cover. Lobby cans had more paper: printed medical results that had been discarded, some used facial tissue, some pages from a personal planner. There were also a couple of soft drink bottles and water bottles. All of it had been fingerprinted or photographed; results would be in the intermediate report.

There was one odd scrap, a very small, yellowish chunk of

a fibrous substance. The map coordinates showed it had been recovered by the leg of a chair near the entrance to the GP practice.

"This doesn't fit," Mason said. "Make a note of the inventory number and look up the photo when we get back."

Cal nodded and made a note.

The second box was fuller. The map that accompanied it was larger, and it contained the map of the entire orthopedic practice, gridded like the lobby map. The CSU team had been thorough in the exam room the victim was found in. They had also been thorough in all the sensible routes from the practice's entrance to that room; the rest of the practice had been given a more cursory look.

Mason and Cal went through all of it and found only the normal detritus of a medical office.

Mason went to the door and waved to Lanny to come back to the room. He appeared in a few seconds. "Whatcha need?"

"This is a medical office with multiple practices. Where is the medical waste? Syringes and things."

"Forgot to mention," Johnson said, "the medical waste — we collected all of it from the orthopedic practice — it requires special handling. Things like needles have pointy parts that no one here wants to get stuck with in the literal sense. There wasn't much of it, by the way. The med waste containers aren't emptied daily, but they *are* on Friday, so all we had was what was administered Monday morning before the alarm sounded."

Mason started to ask something, but Lanny held up a finger, "And before you ask, yes, we are checking all six- and twelve-millimeter needles for anything in the aldehyde family. The M.E. will tell you that the bruising around the site indicates six, but we're checking twelves anyway, since it's the next size up."

"Can you get a list of what was injected? Not who it was injected into, that would be a HIPPA violation." Mason rolled his eyes. "But a list of medications without names should be doable."

"I'll put in the request. If we need a court order, I'll give you a call."

Mason thanked him and he and Cal headed back to their desks. Both stopped off at their restrooms before getting back to their desks. It was now past eleven thirty.

"I'm going to get lunch to bring back," Mason said. "Can I get you anything while I'm out?"

"No, thanks. I brought mine."

12:06 p.m.

Mason made Cal take a break at lunch. "Take a walk, read a book, anything as long as it gets you away from your desk for at least fifteen minutes," he said.

They returned to reading interviews afterward, and traded observations back and forth as they read.

When they got near the end, Mason asked, "Have you seen anything from the lab receptionist?"

"Don't think so," Cal answered.

"Add that to the list. The lab may open early to get blood and other samples for people on the way to work."

"9. Lab receptionist?" appeared on the shared whiteboard program as she typed.

"So what do we want to tackle first?"

Mason said, "I was thinking about that while I was going to get my lunch. We needed to finish the interview reports," he looked at his computer, "that was number one. We went and looked at the physical evidence, that's number six, we'll rate that partial until lab results from the medical waste come in."

He repeatedly tapped his thumb with his forefinger.

"The lab receptionist thing bothers me. Call them, tell them you have a doctor's orders to have blood drawn, find out what their hours are each weekday. Then I want you to go sit in the waiting area and watch the lab reception desk to see what their routine is."

"That seems like a waste of time."

"Yeah. But since no one admitted to being the receptionist, we need to observe the actual practice."

While Cal was calling to find out about lab hours from her personal cell phone (so it couldn't be traced to the police), Mason started on understanding the victim. On his whiteboard program under "3. Victimology" he put several items:

a. Address, phone etc.
b. Previous places lived
c. Bank accounts
d. Credit cards
e. Debts, e.g., car
f. Social habits, friends
g. Relationships, Edward Penfield through Walter Stancill
h. Recent travel
i. Relatives in U.S.
j. Relatives outside U.S.

When he had those items listed, Cal stood up and said,

"Headed to the site." Mason nodded and started filling in what he knew.

Of course, he had the address for Marlene Sauer's apartment already. Her fiancé, Walter Stancill, was already living in her apartment, so he would be treated as a spouse, more or less. Mason put in the request for her financial records and left to see the apartment and hopefully meet him.

2:00 p.m.

Instead of going straight to Marlene Sauer's apartment, Mason first stopped at the apartment complex's leasing office.

The leasing agent, who doubled as the assistant manager for the apartment complex, wore a name tag that read *Nettie*; when Mason asked he learned that her last name was Planer.

"I really don't interact with our residents very much," Nettie said. "At least, not the good ones. I collect and deposit the checks for the residents who still write one."

"And Ms Sauer was one of the good ones?"

"Mm-hm. Rent was always on time." She unconciously twirled one of the blond curls that fell to her jaw line. "She lived here for four years — almost as long as I have worked here. I think she had a roommate when she moved in, but whoever it was left, and she took over the lease entirely."

Mason shifted in his chair, unable to find a comfortable way to sit in it. "Do you get notified about police calls?"

"Sometimes, and sometimes complaints come through me. I try to work with residents, so the police don't have to be called. With Ms Sauer, there was never, ever a complaint about loud music, about arguments, nothing. She did call last week about adding her fiancé to her lease, but the paperwork isn't ready yet."

The agent had almost no personal interaction with the victim, but was sorry to see such a good tenant go, and doubly so because she had died. As part of the application process, the fiancé, Mr Stancill, had been checked, and there were no negatives in his credit report.

2:12 p.m.

The apartment doors were in an alcoves with two doors on the ground floor and two more at the top of a flight of stairs; Marlene's door was upstairs on the right side of the landing. At the door, Mason rang the mechanical bell embedded in the door. When no one answered for a minute, he rang again, then a third time after another minute. When no one answered after that, he decided it was time to canvass the neighbors.

Since he was upstairs anyway, he tried the door on the left. He could hear a blaring television, and thought it was a small-claims court show, the kind where the people "suing" each other have all their expenses paid by the show's producers. A few seconds after he rang the second time, the door opened and Mason was greeted by a sour-faced man, white fringe surrounding his pattern baldness, around seventy-five extra pounds surrounding the middle that poked out beneath his white T-shirt.

"What?" the man grumped. "Who are you?"

Mason held up his badge and introduced himself.

"So what do you want?"

"Have you heard that your neighbor, Ms Sauer, was killed

yesterday?"

"Yes, I heard. Saw it on the morning news. She was killed at work. Whuduz that have ta do with me?"

"Nothing, directly," Mason said. "Can I have your name?"

"I'm Spikes. Jed Spikes."

"Mr Spikes, how well did you know Ms Sauer?"

"Not well. Said hello as we passed. She was pretty and half my age and trim, and I enjoyed watching her come and go." An eyebrow went up. "And her voice was as smooth as silk."

The lecherous old fool, Mason thought.

From behind Jed Spikes came a shrill, "Who's at the door, you ..." ending with an epithet Mason couldn't make out.

A woman of appropriate age and weight to match Mr Spikes and wearing a worn muumuu of purple cotton came up behind him and peered over his shoulder.

"This is a detective," Jed said. "He's trying to learn about Marlene since she died." He pronounced the name correctly.

To Mason he said, "This is my wife of sorts, Colleen."

"This moron," Colleen said, pointing to her husband, "can't get his mind out of the gutter. Just because Marlene" (she pronounced it to rhyme with her own name) "smiles at him and has a pretty shape doesn't mean she's interested in him. Look at him! Who'd be interested in that vast ocean of lard?"

"Look who's talking!" Jed said. "Why I ought —"

"Stop!" Mason interrupted. "I'm not here for your disputes, and if you get much louder, neighbors are going to call officers out here to calm you down. You don't want that, and neither do I."

Both Spikes stood breathing, heavily at first, then lightening to normal.

"But she *was* pretty," Jed said.

"Pretty enough," Colleen begrudged.

Mason let that rest for a second. Then he asked, "How was she as a neighbor? Loud? Always leaving trash by the door? Bringing a lot of men home with her?"

Colleen answered. "When she moved in, she had another woman there, and we thought they might be tangled up, if you know what I mean. But no, they were just roommates in separate bedrooms, with separate hours and separate friends. Her roommate was more social, always inviting people over."

"But they never got too loud or anything," Jed added.

"But sometimes they stayed all night," Colleen kept it going. "The roommate — what was her name? Krysta? Krystal? — she once told me they had too much to drink and slept on the couch rather than drive."

"Seems responsible enough," Mason said. "But Krysta moved out . . ."

"Yeah, that was couple of years back," Colleen said. "Marleen kept the place, and it was really quiet for a while."

"Her name was Mar-LAY-na," Jed said.

Colleen grew more shrill. "She was a foreigner! If she's going to move to America, she should pronounce it like Americans do. Or change the spelling!"

There was an awkward silence for a few seconds.

Mason said, "You said 'really quiet for a while.' What happened?"

Jed said, "Marlene started seeing someone, a man, and after a while *he* started staying the night. Then he quit coming over."

"Do you know his name?"

Both Spikes shook their heads *no*.

"And then?" Mason asked.

Jed said, "Then the present fellow, Walter, started coming around. Never stayed the night. Not until he showed up at the door two or three weeks ago with suitcases. His wife must have thrown him out."

"What's Walter like?"

Coleen said, "Tall. handsome, square jaw, dark hair."

"That's pretty specific."

"That's because I'm looking at him coming up the stairs."

Mason turned to face the man accurately described by his neighbor.

"Mr Stancill, I believe."

"Yes." Walter Stancill said. "And you?"

Mason displayed his badge. "John Mason. I'm so sorry for your loss."

Stancill thanked Mason for his condolences. Mason thanked Jed and Colleen for their help.

Stancill invited him to come inside and unlocked the door.

2:29 p.m.

"How can I help you, Detective? Please, have a seat." He indicated a worn, blue leather sofa.

"I'm looking into Marlene's death," Mason said as he sat. "It appears she was murdered. The case is a very subtle one, and I'm looking for clues in her background. So let's start with something simple: How long have you been engaged?"

On the word 'engaged' Walter suddenly glanced directly at Mason's face.

"Engaged. Yes, I guess we were. My wife helped me leave the house a couple of weeks ago with sharp and pointed words

I won't repeat for you. We've argued over women before, but when she became so angry that I thought she might follow up the words with sharp and pointed instruments, I decided she was serious.

"Marlene and I had been seeing each other romantically for a couple of months. And yes, before you ask, we were ... intimate. So when I came here with suitcases, Marlene took me in on the condition that it be a permanent arrangement. Eventually, we would have married. After my divorce, of course."

Mason said, "I understand Marlene had put in notice at work."

"Sure. I'm pretty well off, so I told her she didn't have to work if she didn't want to. She was unhappy at work, so she gave them notice."

"Do you know why she was unhappy at work?"

"It had something to do with one of the doctors, I think. She — the doctor — had become too friendly, bumping into Marlene the wrong way, smiling at her anatomy rather than her face the way an employer or friend would. The atmosphere with that doctor was borderline ... hostile, but there was nothing overt Marlene could point to for legal action. And after a break, she could have gone to work at any orthopedic practice in metro Atlanta."

"The doctor's name?"

"German, ironically."

"Marlene's name was German, what was special about this doctor?"

"I mean her name was the word 'German.' Even more ironically, her first name is Irene."

"Huh?" After a second Mason shook his head. "I'm usually the one who makes those jokes," he said as he wrote it all down.

"How about Marlene's family in Germany? I know she moved to the U.S. for nursing school, and she stayed afterward when she met someone."

"Yeah, I never met him. They divorced a long time ago. I think she was sad about that, but I never got the full story."

So I know more about that than you, Mason thought. "Back to relatives?"

"I've never met any of them; I think they're all in Germany," Walter said. "And I've only lived here for a couple of weeks, so we never got around to that. It'll be somewhere in her papers. She was a meticulous record keeper."

"I need to send someone around to pick those up this evening. Will you be here?"

"I had a meeting," Stancill said, "but don't have the heart for it now, so yes, I'll be here. Can you send someone before, say, eight thirty?"

"No problem. Someone will be here by eight."

"Marlene kept everything in a two-drawer file cabinet, so you'll either need to take the whole thing or bring file boxes."

"Again, no problem. I appreciate your cooperation."

Mason rose to leave, and Walter started to get up as well.

"No need to get up," Mason said, and Walter fell back into his seat.

On his way down the stairs, Mason muttered, "Poor guy, alone and no home to go to. I bet his own family disowned him long ago."

He had purposely avoided mentioning that Patricia, Walter's (probable) ex-wife, worked in the same building as Marlene. He stopped at the bottom of the stairs and wrote in his pad, *Walter is well off. Why is Patricia working at a doctor's office?*

3:43 p.m.

On his way back to the station, Mason swung by the Booker Medical Building to see whether Cal was still installed there.

He was approaching the door as Cal exited. Rather than entering, he met her at her Jeep. He leaned against an adjacent car as she explained.

"The lab doesn't have a real receptionist. There's a sign-in pad at the reception desk. People getting lab work done write down their name, the time, and the name of the doctor who put in the orders. Then they sit and wait until the next available tech comes along and calls them in for whatever needs to be done."

"So it's not a surprise that someone could get into the lab halls, and presumably out, as well, without being seen. What are their hours of operation?"

"Monday and Thursday, they start at six thirty. Other weekdays, the earliest they'll see anyone is seven forty-five. Oh, and eight to noon on Saturday."

Mason acknowledged her work and outlined what he had learned from Walter Stancill and his neighbors. "And if Patricia Stancill is his wife, we need to make sure her alibi holds up."

"Next up?" Cal asked.

"Go to the station and get a uniformed officer to go with you to pick up Marlene's papers. Get two or three file storage boxes and expense them. Or see what you can wheedle out of forensics. Take it back to evidence, but don't look at anything until we have a court order."

"And then?"

"Then go home. I'll put in the request for the court order. Be back in the morning at seven thirty. If the warrant has come in, start on Marlene's personal papers. Look for relatives in Europe we need to contact. We'll need to get that done early because it will have been two days, and they're six hours ahead of us."

7:07 p.m.

At the Mason home, Tuesday was lo mein night. John and his wife, Ann Fleming, got a large carton of cheap lo mein and had beer or wine to drink. It was a sort of unofficial meeting time, flexible to meet the weirdness in their schedules. As a detective, John couldn't guarantee a night, and Ann's work as a high-end residential real estate broker could have her out at all hours. Sometimes their Tuesday meeting was as late as Saturday, but this week, they hit their target day.

Ann described the two clients she had seen on Monday and Tuesday. The Monday client was looking to sell a little shack she estimated would go for seven and a half million; the Tuesday client was looking for something that wasn't on the market at the moment. But Ann knew half a dozen properties that fit and would go looking tomorrow to see if any of them were interested in selling.

John told Ann about his conversations with Lilia (even though, or rather especially because his current wife needed to know about his contact with his ex-wife) and with Ron Penfield.

"How *are* Ron and Clarissa?" Ann asked. "I hated to miss the wedding, but that Saturday was a busy day."

"They seemed very, very happy."

"And you said they were at home?"

"Yep, alone."

"Newlyweds with the house to themselves," Ann mocked. "I can't imagine *why* they would want that!" More seriously, she said, "But why go see Ron?"

Mason chewed and swallowed an overcooked shrimp and some noodles, chased them down with a sip of his drink, and said, "Because his brother was in the building when Marlene Sauer was killed."

"Coincidence?"

"Worse: Ed Penfield was the victim's ex-husband. Coincidence? You tell me. But that's not all: Ed had gone there explicitly to talk with her. Which he did, until they were interrupted by the fire alarm, according to him."

"Was he trying to get back together with her?" Ann asked as she fished a noodle out of the carton with her chopsticks.

"Again, according to him, he's in a recovery program, and he hit the step where he apologizes to those he's hurt. And she recently got engaged and put in notice she was leaving her job."

"Her fiancé must be in good shape if she could leave her job."

"Apparently, yeah," John said digging for more shrimp on his turn with the carton. "He was living with her, getting put onto her lease. Was surprised by the word 'engaged,' but supposed it was inevitable. He said his wife kicked him out."

"A warning all married men should heed," Ann said both lightly and seriously.

"Yes, dear," John said in his best Caspar Milquetoast voice.

"What's his name? The fiancé?"

"Walter Stancill."

Ann sat back in her chair, eyes wide. "Really? *Walter* Stancill?"

"Have you heard of him?"

"Heard of him?" Ann asked. "I sold him his house in Arcadia Commons. And it's not the smallest place in there. And he paid cash."

"Yikes," John said. "Do you remember his wife?"

Ann thought for a moment, then nodded. "Yes. She was short, petite, short blond hair. I think she did something athletic — running? No ... Ballet? No ..." She grabbed a short breath. "Gymnastics. That was it. She does adult gymnastics as a hobby. She worked as an RN."

The description matches the nurse, he thought. "Any idea why she would be working rather than enjoying the high life?"

"Some people have a compulsion to work. Walter, as I recall, tried to pick me up once when it was just him and me. After that, I wouldn't meet with him without ... Pat? Patty ... without Patty there."

It was John's turn to be both light and serious. "And as your husband, I appreciate that."

Ann got the last noodle from the carton. "You know," she said with a flirty grin, twirling the noodle around the end of her chopsticks, "Ron and Clarissa shouldn't be the only happy couple in town."

"And still as your husband," John repeated, "I appreciate that even more."

They both gulped their remaining wine and left the carton, the chopsticks, and the wine glasses on their own recognizance for a while.

Wednesday, November 7

6:45 a.m.

At a quarter to seven the next morning, Ann had just left for work. Mason's cell phone rang as he put the wine glasses from the previous night into the dishwasher. There were a couple of days' dishes in there, so he answered his phone as he put a detergent packet in.

His phone's screen indicated the call came from the police station.

"Mason."

"Hey, John," Catherine Caligari said. "Hope I didn't wake you."

"Naw, it's just the dishwasher won't be started for a minute. Why so early?"

The day before he had said seven thirty.

"Couldn't sleep," Cal said. "Got to the office an hour ago," (Mason winced at the thought of being there at five forty-five) "and the court order for the victim's papers had come through."

"Sooo … you wouldn't be calling me if you didn't have something already."

"Yes, sir. Our victim was in good shape, financially. Alimony was regular, but only about half of what she needed to live on. She owned her car outright and had pretty sizable savings in both retirement and money market accounts."

"So she was sensible. Anything else?"

"She has been talking with real estate agents, getting a feel for the housing market."

"Hm. Walter might have a different way of thinking about that."

"Why?" Cal asked.

"Because the house his wife threw him out of was in Arcadia Commons."

"Wow. Is she still living there?"

"Presumably," Mason said. "We may have to visit, just to see what the lawyers will be squabbling over."Got any line on relatives to contact?"

"Not yet."

"Try looking for life insurance, foreign correspondence, anything like that. Relatives may be listed there."

"Will do."

They rang off, and Mason started the dishwasher.

8:00 a.m.

"Sergio!" Mason called as Lieutenant Tejeda was passing by on his way to his office.

Tejeda diverted to Mason's desk. He nodded to Cal.

"What do you need, Detective?"

"Our victim, Marlene Sauer, was a naturalized U.S. citizen; her family is in Germany. I need authorization for an international call to notify next of kin."

Tejeda said, "Shouldn't be a problem, but I'll check with the captain. What can I report to him for you?"

Mason outlined the case: the fire alarm, the injection, the ex-husband, the boyfriend's wife, the small amount of physical evidence. The lieutenant had heard parts of it late Monday, but the full update filled in details Captain Berman would want.

Tejeda nodded and went off to relay it all to the captain.

As Walter had told Mason the night before, Marlene Sauer's papers were well organized. And when Cal and the officer had transferred everything to file boxes, they had preserved the order well. Points to the new detective.

Marlene had lived comfortably, but within her means. In addition to the finances Cal had perused that morning, they found that Marlene Sauer always paid off her credit cards; paid her other bills (electricity, cable, cell phone; not water or sewer since they were included in her rent) on time; ate out around twice a week; bought groceries weekly; bought clothes quarterly; always bought gasoline at the same station; rarely seemed to use cash.

She had a moderate life insurance policy, with a beneficiary of Lukas Sauer, who had an address in Leipzig, Germany. A phone number was also given. Mason noted this down and kept working.

While Marlene had still been married to Ed Penfield, she had given up her nursing career when she became pregnant; after their divorce, she had lived on alimony and ramen while she got her nursing credentials renewed, after which she moved to Atlanta.

In Atlanta, Marlene had worked for a couple of different medical practices as an orthopedic nurse. She had copies of her performance reviews from her employers, and she always rated in one of the top two tiers (out of four or five).

Cal found that about seven weeks back, her spending patterns had changed a little. Mason guessed it was around the time she had started seeing Walter Stancill.

Judging from some of her older credit card statements, she had been involved with at least one man prior to her most recent attachment to Walter.

"A simple, quiet life," Cal said when Mason asked her for a summary. "No indications of drug use or alcohol abuse. No mountain of debt that might make her scout out a rich guy like Stancill."

"How about her computer?" Mason asked.

"That's with the specialists. Stancill gave us the password, so there was no trickery involved trying to guess."

"Convenient. Just so you know: When we have the password and the appropriate warrant, we can go ahead and examine it ourselves."

"Sorry." Cal looked down at her desk.

"Not a problem," Mason said. "It wasn't a reprimand. The forensics people would have gotten it from us anyway, and this way they will give us a table of contents to use as a guide when we do get it. And we have plenty to keep us busy until they finish with it."

Cal looked back up at him. "Okay. How about I go through her phone records?"

8:12 a.m.

"Great idea. I'm going to go through the physical evidence again."

Rather than going downstairs to the forensics lab right away, Mason pulled up the crime scene reports and photos. He printed copies of the two floor plans so he could point to the associated grid square for each item as he looked at the report and the photos.

"What's missing?" he muttered to himself. He almost reflexively replied, "Where's the syringe?"

He paged through the report looking for information about the medical waste the forensics folks were analyzing. Some of the analysis had been completed, and it showed nothing startling. All the syringes in the waste had been examined, and none contained anything in the aldehyde family. They would still be matched up with the records of what had been dispensed Monday morning, but there was almost no hope of turning up anything he needed.

"Rats," Mason said.

"Mice," Cal replied. "What's wrong?"

"We have a first-degree murder, and the perp walked out of the building with the weapon."

"If this was all that premeditated, all the killer had to do was dispose of that syringe somewhere out of the way, say, a convenience store trash can, where no one will look."

"Probably somewhere preplanned, to take the guesswork out," Mason agreed.

"Because the adrenaline rush would make thinking after the fact hard," Cal added.

Mason completed the thought. "And a lot of people would make a mistake under pressure."

"So the planner had to be both audacious and meticulous."

They fell silent as Mason stared at his computer monitor without seeing it.

8:36 a.m.

Tejeda came through and gave Mason the goahead to make the international phone call to Marlene Sauer's next of kin.

Mason riffled through his notes to find the number for Lukas Sauer and punched in the digits, which came in different groupings from U.S. phone numbers. After several ratchety-sounding rings, someone picked up.

"*Ja. Sauer.*" Male voice, medium pitch.

"Hello." Mason paused a couple of seconds to give the person answering a second to (hopefully) switch gears into English. "My name is John Mason, and I'm calling from the United States to speak to Lukas Sauer."

"*Ja* — yes, this is Lukas Sauer." He paused slightly, looking for the correct English phrase. "How may I help you?"

"Mr Sauer, I'm a policeman in Bristow, Georgia, near Atlanta. I understand you have a relative in the U.S. named Marlene Sauer."

"Yes, that is correct. Marlene is my sister. Is she . . . okay?"

Mason always hated this part, especially when he had to do it on a phone call. "No, I'm afraid she is not okay. She was killed two days ago."

There was a long pause.

"Was Marlene killed in an accident?"

"No, sir. She was murdered."

"Where was she killed? Was it on your streets? Or in a parking lot?"

Reasonable guesses, Mason thought. *But no.* "Marlene was killed in the medical clinic she worked in." He briefly explained how her death occurred, leaving out (for now) Ed Penfield, Walter Stancill, and other circumstances.

"It appears you were her next of kin, Mr Sauer. That means that when our medical examiner has completed all his work, we will need you to take responsibility for her body."

"*Ich verstehe.* I understand. I will need —" He paused, and Mason thought he could hear the muffled sound of the mouthpiece or microphone being covered. And sobbing.

After a moment, Lukas spoke again. "*Entschuldegen* ... I apologize. ... Anyway, I will need to arrange for time away from work, and I will need a flight to Atlanta. I can send you my travel plans through electronic ... email."

Mason gave his contact information and told Lukas he would reply to his email with a list of hotels in the area. He offered his condolences, hoping his words would be understood as he intended. They rang off.

The detectives spent the remainder of the morning going through the papers of the victim.

11:30 a.m.

While Cal was eating her lunch — high in protein and vegetables, low in carbs, Mason noticed — Mason went for a walk. He walked the couple of blocks to the main square downtown, then circled the square a couple of times, not paying any attention to the shops or restaurants, only heeding foot and motor traffic enough to avoid accidents.

12:01 p.m.

Back at his desk, Mason told Cal, "Here's something I learned at home last night. Patricia Stancill, who works in the GP office, is indeed Walter Stancill's wife. And they parted on unfriendly terms."

"You told me about the parting. But how did you find out at home?"

"My wife was the broker when Stancill bought the mansion."

"So we have someone in the building who presumably has motive, but no opportunity," Cal concluded, "because she works as far from the victim as you can get."

"And Marlene had an ex-husband already talking to her — right there *in the room* with her — who presumably has no motive." Mason looked up at Cal. "Find out who in the prosecutor's office is assigned to this. Call and ask whoever it is to request a court order in Amory, Mississippi for financials and communication records on Ed Penfield. We have to find out about motive."

Cal picked up her phone to call, and Mason motioned that he was headed downstairs to forensics.

12:10 p.m.

Mason entered the forensics department by the stairwell as usual.

But when Lanny Johnson saw him, there was no exchange of banter. Lanny could tell Mason wasn't in the mood for it.

"Can I have the exam room?" Mason asked without even saying *hi.*

"Sure," Lanny said. "Mind if I come along?"

"If you want."

In the room, Mason got the box of items from inside the orthopedic practice and spread everything out on the tables, roughly approximating the layout of the office. The syringes from the medical waste containers had been put in hard plastic sleeves to prevent accidental punctures, and they were labeled with the contents and the location of the bin they were recovered from.

"Are you any closer to identifying the poison?"

Lanny said, "Yes, just added that to the report on the server and was about to call when you appeared. One of my people used to be a medical lab tech, and she put us on to what to test for. It's called glutaraldehyde; it's used as a disinfectant on surgical instruments. Comes in gallon bottles. Sometimes used to treat warts, but externally. Inside the body: bad news. Very bad."

"Definitely and purposely injected, but no syringe found that contained it." After a moment, Mason said, "You'll hate me for this. Go back to the building, find every bottle of the stuff in there that has been opened, and check for prints. I'll send someone to interview staff about unexpectedly open bottles. And we still don't have a syringe."

"So someone walked with it."

"Yeah," Mason muttered. "Yeah. But pick up the medical waste again and check all that's accumulated since. If they pocketed it and then brought it back for disposal ..."

"Where it wouldn't be noticed," Johnson finished. "Got it."

Returning to his desk, Mason told Cal, "I'm going out for a while. Call if anything important happens."

She nodded abstractedly — she was going through reports and interviews again — and he left.

12:12 p.m.

"Ron, please don't hang up." Ed Penfield was pleading, almost desperate.

"Why not?" Ron stood in his kitchen as Clarissa prerpared lunch.

"Look, I need to talk with you."

"Part of your *program*?" Ron spat out.

Ed sighed audibly. "Yes, it's part of the program. But it's also true."

Ron paused long enough to make Ed wonder whether his brother would reject him totally.

"Fine," Ron said. He looked at the clock on the microwave. "Meet me at one thirty at the Great Northwest on 128. They can give you directions at your hotel desk. But don't expect much."

Ron rang off angrily and began pacing the tile floor between the oak cabinets.

As Ron was talking with Ed, Clarissa set a bowl of chips and a small bowl of guacamole to share on the table and got them ice water to drink.

"Ed?" she asked.

"Yeah. I'm going to meet him this afternoon."

"I heard. And then?"

"I'll hear what he has to say," Ron said, "then I'll come home."

"What will you *do* with what he says? Will you believe him?"

"I doubt it."

Clarissa pursed her lips and rested her hands on the tile surface of the island. When she spoke, she said, "I think you should give him a chance."

"Why? What did he do to deserve a *chance*?"

Clarissa's voice sank to a whisper. What was it they read this morning? She could hear Ron's own voice reading it to her as she repeated it. " 'Be kind to one another, tenderhearted, forgiving one another, as God in Christ forgave you.' Why did *we* deserve a chance, O husband of mine?"

Ron stared into Clarissa's eyes, angry with Ed for waiting so long, angry with Clarissa for being right, angry with ... himself.

Yeah, angry with himself.

He sighed; he slouched in his chair; his shoulders drooped; his eyelids drooped.

"You're right," he whispered as he sat.

He sat still like that for a few minutes.

"Now," Clarissa said as the toaster oven dinged, "eat your lunch. Forgiving is hard work." She sliced her sandwich and Ron's diagonally and set their plates so they were eating across the corner of the table.

Ron sat up. For a couple of minutes, they ate in silence.

Several bites into his sandwich, Ron said, "This is wonderful. What did you do?"

"Bread I made in the bread machine, roast beef, brown mustard, mayo, some bacon crumbles, bits of sun-dried tomato, grated cheese blend. Put the mustard and beef on one slice of bread, the mayo and crumbly stuff on the other slice. Warm in the toaster oven until the cheese gets melty. Put it together and toast until toasted; cut diagonally."

"This is the best sandwich I've had in months."

"Thank you." Clarissa smiled. After a moment she was bemused. "I don't know —"

"— Stop right there," Ron interrupted. He held up a forefinger. "No comparison."

"No comparison," Clarissa agreed, grateful for his understanding.

1:30 p.m.

Mason went to Booker Medical Building and sat in the waiting room near the building entrance but facing the center of the room so he could watch the comings and goings at every practice and at the lab.

The lab operated as Cal had described to him: no real receptionist, and different techs came to get names from the check-in register. Presumably, they'd go and prep whatever they were doing next, then come and call the patient.

The medical practices operated differently: A receptionist was at the desk full time, directing people to the check-in log, getting insurance information, taking payments, answering the phone.

After half an hour in his observation post, he approached the orthopedic desk. The receptionist recognized him at once.

"Detective Mason!" Ruby said. "How can I help you?"

"I was hoping to wander your halls for a few minutes," Mason said. "I don't want to disrupt anything, just to try to get a feel for this as a . . . a *place.* Do you think I can do that?"

"That shouldn't be a problem," Ruby said. "This business has us all mystified. All four doctors have told us to cooperate as fully as we can, as long as all our patients are cared for."

"I appreciate that."

"Just let me know when you're leaving so I can take you off the emergency list."

"Thanks." Mason's eyes narrowed. "One question before I start: On Monday, Ed Penfield wasn't on the emergency list, but you're being careful to add me to it. What was different on Monday?"

"Well," Ruby said, looking down, seeming embarrassed, voice softening to almost a whisper, "he wasn't here, officially. The staff aren't supposed to have personal visitors, and I didn't want to get Marlene in trouble in her next to last week. It's really my fault."

As Mason opened the door to go into the hallway, he thought, *If it goes badly for Ed Penfield, she may have to admit that in court.*

What Mason found in the practice wasn't very revealing: Exam rooms, nurses' work area with nurses coming and going and working at computers, a couple of restrooms, storage closets, a small records room. There was one enclosed office for the office manager; a nameplate on the closed door read *Jacquiline Shelb.*

The hallways in the practice were indeed a perplexing network, and even though Mason had seen the floor plan, he still got turned around trying to explore.

He found the exam room Marlene Sauer's body had been discovered in. He had requested that the room not be used for at least a week; at the request of the practice for the comfort of the patients, no crime scene tape had been affixed to the door frame. So he wasn't surprised when the door was locked. He found his way back to Ms Shelb's office and knocked.

A call of "Enter" came through the door, and he complied.

Jacquiline Shelb appeared to be in her mid thirties with very short, light brown hair, and dressed in a white shirt with a Nehru collar and a dark, collarless suit that covered a frame that was wide but not thick.

"Detective," she said, her voice naturally pitched low, "what can I help you with?"

"I was hoping to get a look at the room where Ms Sauer's body was found. Do you have the key, or should I ask someone else?"

"I have it right here," she said. "I have been wondering whether you might come by for it."

He thanked her and promised to put the key under the door if she wasn't there when he was ready to return it.

Except for the absence of the body, the room was unchanged. Mason moved everything in the room that could be moved; looked in every drawer, every cubbyhole; poked around in a tissue box and in a box of exam gloves, throwing away any glove or tissue he touched; looked at all the supplies. He knew he wouldn't find anything — the CSU team was very good. Except ...

Except he did find one thing: Behind a wheel of the exam table, he found another piece of the strange fibrous material he had looked at in the forensic exam room. He labeled an evidence bag and pushed the object into the bag with a pen.

So that was that. Mason relocked the door, returned the key to Ms Shelb, and tried to find his way back out from memory. He finally gave up and followed the exit signs. *Ed Penfield may have very well told us the truth about getting lost. The fire alarm sounding would be disorienting.*

Mason sat in the waiting area again for a few minutes. Then he went back to the station and reread reports for the rest of the workday.

1:30 p.m.

Ron and Ed sat in a corner in the Great Northwest Coffee Emporium and Meeting Room and looked at each other, not talking, until their orders were ready. Ron had gotten a pour over of Jamaica Blue Mountain; Ed's was a huge cappuccino into which he mixed a little honey and onto which he sprinkled some cinnamon.

"You know why I wanted to meet," Ed said.

"And you know why I didn't," Ron snapped.

"And I can't blame you." Deep breath. "After Cory died, I couldn't handle it. To be a little diagnostic about it after the fact, I self-sedated so I wasn't *able* to think about him. And at Dad's funeral ..." Tears streamed down Ed's face. "I'm so, so sorry ... I'm sorry about being drunk at Dad's funeral; I'm sorry about *missing* Barb's — she was so great."

A tear escaped Ron's eye. "Yeah, she was." He sipped his coffee.

"I know you didn't want me there, but I'm glad I was at your wedding. Clarissa was a lighthouse wherever she smiled." Ed drank some of his cappuccino.

"Yeah, she's great, too." Ron shook his head slowly, lost in thought. "Did you ever wonder what to wish for?"

"Wha'da'yah mean?"

Ron chewed his lip. "I mean, until a few months ago, I would have given anything, *everything*, to have Barb back. But now ... I never want to give Clarissa up. I almost feel *guilty* for letting go of Barb."

"She's gone, bro," Ed said softly. "Just like Marlene's gone. I was talking with her when the fire alarm sounded. I think ... Her mouth was just starting to move, and I can hope ... wish ... no, I *hope* she was about to say she was forgiving me."

They both sipped their coffees before Ed continued.

"And I hope you can. Nothing I do — nothing *anyone* can do will make up for what I've done to you — what I've done to the whole family. I know that. But only you can forgive me."

That hung in the air for five minutes.

And then for a couple more. They drank in silence.

When Ron finished his Blue Mountain, he glanced at Ed, then through the window, then looked at Ed.

"My wife," Ron said, "told me to listen to you. And in the Bible, God told me to forgive. As my wife reminded me at lunchtime."

Ron concluded, "I forgive you Ed."

Ed, consoled and comforted, sobbed.

"You know," Ron said, "it's going to take me a while to adjust to this. I'll have to fight with myself to even be civil with you."

"I'll take it," Ed said, drying his face on a napkin. "Be right back," he said, walking toward the restroom.

While Ed was gone, Ron called Clarissa. "It's done," he said. "Is it okay if I invite Ed to dinner?"

6:30 p.m.

That evening, as Ed Penfield was arriving at Ron and Clarissa's house, and as Mason was getting a dinner salad to take back to his desk (Ann had a client that would keep her tied up late), Lilia and Adena were sitting down to eat. As usual Adena was examining the grain of the wooden tabletop.

"I saw your father yesterday, Adena."

"How was Daddy?"

"He seemed fine. We did not get to talk about personal matters; he was there on police business."

"Is he investigating the death at the clinic on Monday?"

"Yes."

"I could not work out how to pronounce her name. Was she an American?"

"Like me, she was a naturalized citizen. She was originally from Germany. Her name was pronounced Mar-LAY-na Sour."

"Sour grapes. Sour note. Sour stomach. The newspaper said she was engaged to Walter."

"Yes."

"Did you know her?"

"We said hello sometimes. I do not think she knew that I knew Walter."

"Walter was always polite."

Lilia could tell that Adena wanted to say more. "Yes, but what else?"

"He was *only* polite to me. Like he had to be, not like he wanted to."

"He did not understand extraordinary people." Lilia thought, *Not besides himself.* "He made his living — a very good living — working with people who *were* ordinary. He could not work out how to be more than courteous with you."

Adena waited a minute before asking, "What kind of fire alarm do you have at work?"

Lilia was glad to change the subject. "It is a very loud bell that rings rapidly until someone outside the building turns it off. We leave it ringing until the last person has left the building."

"How do you know when everyone is out?"

"Do you remember how our building is divided?"

Still Adena attended to the grain of the table. "There are four sections."

"That is right. Each section has appointed someone to check all the rooms and make sure they are empty. In the part of the building that I work in, *I* am that person."

"And when you have checked a room, you move the tag to the side where you can see it in the hall, so you don't have to check that room again."

"Just so."

Something started to bother Lilia. "Except ..." she whispered. Worry caused her face to scrunch up. "I had already ..." She shook her head, brown tresses waving. "Why would that door open if ...?" She realized what was bothering her. She would need to check on it at work tomorrow.

7:02 p.m.

At the Penfield house, conversation was restrained, but it relaxed as they consumed Clarissa's excellent and hearty beef stew in the kitchen. It was just the thing for a cold autumn evening. "Eating in the kitchen will make it seem more like family," Clarissa had said. She served water and iced tea even for Ron and herself, out of deference to Ed's alcoholism.

Young Ed and Lenna were there, of course. Gloria, Ron's first mother-in-law, was still away. Ronny — Ron Jr — would be joining them in a little while, as he had a late weight-training session; he was a walk-on on his college baseball team.

Lenna — properly called Elena — sort of remembered Uncle Ed. Ed, named after Uncle Ed before he started drinking heavily — barely remembered him. Both sat and listened as Ed caught Ron up on happenings from home. Ed lived and worked in Amory, Mississippi, but the brothers had grown up about thirty-five miles away in Houston.

Young Ed sourly whispered to Lenna that Grandma — he meant Gloria — was in a very different Houston. "Grandma's is about a thousand times as big," Lenna whispered back.

"So what is small-town law practice like?" Clarissa asked. They were about halfway through dinner.

"Not much like the TV shows," Ed said. "I handle wills and other probate matters, contracts, the occasional drunk driver. Lately, meaning the last eight years or so, I've been getting more drug charges — marijuana and meth, mostly. I have one case that's pending for heroin possession, but I'm going to try to get my client to see reason and negotiate supervised outpatient methadone rehab."

"What would be the alternative?" Clarissa asked.

"Multiple years in the state prison at Parchman. It has a reputation as a hellhole." Ed took a swallow of tea. "A while back a couple of people wanted to sue the paper mill, but they wound up paying me to talk them out of it."

"So it's like the town I grew up in," Clarissa said, "just with different employers. But people go to work, some go to church, and some party hard."

"And some party hard and go to church anyway," Ron said, glancing sharply at Ed. Then his head dropped in shame. "Sorry. Old habit."

Ed sighed. "I understand." After a few seconds, he continued. "Like you said this afternoon, it will take time."

Stepmom and daughter, with grudging help from son, started clearing dishes to ready the table for dessert.

Ed greeted Ron Jr as he came in. He had already had dinner, but he gratefully accepted the offer of dessert. He was still breathing deep from his training session.

"So," Ron Jr said to Ed, "how fast did you drive to get over here from Amory?"

"Drive? I didn't drive," Ed said. Everyone's head swiveled around to look at him. "It had been raining, so I just got up to speed, and around the time I hit the Alabama line, I jammed on the brakes and slid the rest of the way on the wet kudzu. Passed two highway patrolmen in Alabama who couldn't keep up."

Everyone laughed. When Ron recovered, he asked, "Do you ever think they'll be able to get rid of it? The kudzu?"

"Nope. Do you remember that old anthology film, *Dr Terror's House of Horrors*? The creeping vine story was inspired by kudzu — I'm convinced of it."

They all laughed again. "So," Ron Jr asked when he finished laughing, "why are you in town?"

Ron, Ed, and Clarissa looked around the table at each other, awkwardly.

"I . . ." Ed started.

He tried again. "I came . . ." He choked up. He closed his

eyes and took a deep breath.

"Do you remember how I didn't come to your mom's funeral?" He glanced at Clarissa to make sure it would be okay. She nodded, and he went on.

"I don't know what your dad told you, but he was probably trying to protect you from knowing."

Bumper said, "He said you were out of the country."

"I wasn't," Ed said. "I was . . . too . . . I was out, all right, but out of my mind, drunk. I was drunk at our dad's funeral, too, just not as bad."

Lenna asked, "Why were you drinking so much?"

"You won't remember, but when I was married to Marlene, we had a little boy. Cory . . . died . . . cancer. I drank to forget."

Everyone was silent, absorbing Ed's confession.

"And I came . . . to ask your dad . . . all of you . . . to . . . forgive me." He closed his eyes and his face twisted as he tried to prevent the tears from flooding.

"For my part," Ron said as they absorbed this, "Ed and I already talked, and I did . . . I *am* forgiving him."

"So, um," Ron said after a minute, "how long have you been sober?"

"Six months and five days," Ed said. "And just so you know, these have not all been easy days. There are times when the desire . . . the longing . . . the craving . . ."

"The jonesing," Young Ed said.

Everyone looked at him.

"What? It's common slang."

"And you used it correctly," Ron said.

Ed went on. "Sometimes I can't eat at a restaurant when I know they serve even just wine or beer. I eat too much fast food now. Sometimes, I can manage someplace where alcohol is served. But not always."

Lenna said, "So you had a little boy, what happened to … your … ohhh." Her eyes widened to huge circles.

"What?" Young Ed and Ron Jr said at the same time.

Lenna whispered, "She was … "

"Yes," Ed said. "Marlene left me when I was drinking. She was the woman who was killed Monday at the doctor's office. I may have been the last person to see her alive, except for the person who killed her."

Ron and Clarissa knew this already; all the kids were stunned.

"And the police have requested that I stay in town."

Why? hung over the table, but no one asked. Ed answered it anyway.

"Because I'm a suspect."

9:01 p.m.

"Hey, John." Cal breathed heavily between words.

"Did I interrupt something?" Mason asked; he was driving home, phone connected to his car via Bluetooth.

"No." She panted a couple of times. "I just finished practicing with my partner." More panting. "Wait, you don't know. A friend and I are a beach volleyball duo. We started out at the bottom of our league a couple of seasons ago, but we're getting better."

"That answers more than one question," Mason said. "But I'm calling about tomorrow."

Cal was regaining her breath. She gulped down some water and said, "What's up tomorrow?"

"I need you to dress up a little. We're going to the rarified atmosphere of Arcadia Commons."

"Should I bring my own oxygen?"

Cal couldn't see it, but Mason smiled at that.

"No, we won't go the upper floors of the house. Just be ready to leave the station at nine a.m."

"Will do. What should I wear? I mean like, dressy pants or a skirt or a dress or a suit?"

Mason considered. "The suit is too much. Wear the pants. It may keep Patricia Stancill from putting up her guard."

"Won't she be at work?"

"I got the duty roster from the doctor's office, and she has scheduled half a day off. I called her, and she said we could come by around nine thirty."

"What will be our line of attack?" Cal asked.

"Information gathering. But we'll talk specifics on the way there."

"Sounds good."

Thursday, November 8

9:20 a.m.

Calling Arcadia Commons a wealthy neighborhood was like calling lions or sharks predators. The houses — mansions — provided meaning and purpose to tracts of five to ten acres; driveways variously wound or plunged through woods of oak or hickory or pine or, in one degenerate case that required hiring harvesters, pecan. The largest of the houses covered half an acre and stood two stories, except where it stood three.

Mason and Cal were admitted at the Commons gate by a guard who seemed competent to use the firearm at his side. As they departed the gate shack, Cal asked, "Do you think he has a permit for that?"

"Yep. I've met him. He's ex-Army and working his way through law school."

They drove on along the groves, separated from the trees by fences of brick or iron or stone with the occasional gate affording a glimpse up a driveway, and sometimes a peek at a rooftop or a colonnaded, two- or three-story porch.

As they reached the address indicated, the iron gate began to open.

"Either it's haunted or we're expected," Mason said.

"I vote for B," Cal laughed.

They drove up to the house through a grove of about a hundred and fifty well-tended peach trees, and parked to the right of the steps leading up to the front porch on a driveway that arced past the ten-foot high, double front doors. A broad, grassy area before the door would serve as parking space for large parties.

"We're kind of far north for peach trees," Mason said. "The soil here is wrong."

Cal nodded.

When they exited the car, Cal smoothed the legs of her pants. She wore high heels, bringing her up to Mason's height, and Mason noticed that she moved gracefully in them, like a dancer or a gymnast might. Ann, Mason's wife, had always been grateful for being taller than average, and thus not requiring heels for most occasions.

Mason, uncharacteristically wearing a tie, got his sport coat from a hanger behind his seat.

Cal was a step or two ahead and rang the bell when she reached the door. Mason stopped beside her and said, "You clean up pretty good."

"The sooner I'm out of the monkey suit and back in work clothes, the happier I'll be."

The door was opened by a maid who was slender, with dark brown skin, short black hair, and was dressed in black denim jeans and a blue chambray shirt. "Detective Mason?"

Mason nodded. "And this is Detective Caligari."

"I'm happy to meet you. My name is Idell." She pronounced

her name eye-DELL. "Would you follow me?"

They followed her through an entry hall that might serve as a small reception room. Flooring was white marble tiles; walls were papered with cloth depicting African wildlife silhouetted in a barely contrasting color, though if you didn't look carefully, you wouldn't notice the animals; a four-foot-high by eight-foot-wide mirror stood above a long, dark cherry table topped with black marble; a large central vase with fresh roses was flanked by smaller ewers of white carnations.

Idell led them into a small — relatively small — room lined with bookshelves. Mason supposed this might be called a library.

"Please have a seat. Mrs Stancill will be here soon."

"I'm here, Idell."

Patricia Stancill, all of five feet, two inches, slender, dressed in silver-gray linen pants and house jacket, the latter over a light navy tunic, and ballet flats stepped around Idell and held out a hand to Mason. "Detectives," she said, "I'm Patty Stancill. You are . . . ?"

"John Mason, and this is Detective Catherine Caligari."

"Can I offer you coffee or tea?"

Cal said, "Tea would be lovely, thank you." En route, Mason had suggested that she accept tea or coffee if it was offered. He said that people instinctively trust people they do favors for, at least when you don't have a track record of blowing their trust.

Mason said, "Nothing for me, thanks."

"I'll have tea as well," Patty said to Idell.

Idell nodded and backed around her employer. The detectives sat in chairs, Patty took a position near the center of the sofa.

"Now, detectives, how can I help you?"

"You may recall we were at the scene on Monday after Marlene Sauer was killed."

"Ah, that's what this is about. I wish I had something to contribute to your investigation. Ms Sauer worked in a different practice than mine. I didn't see her Monday morning, since I was in the back in the exam rooms and nurses' station until the alarm sounded."

"Sure," Mason said, "we are aware you work in the General Practice. And you were on the surveillance video of the waiting area entering that office for work, and around the time of the alarm you only reentered the waiting area to leave the building after the alarm sounded."

"And," Cal chimed in, "there are no communicating doors that would get you from the waiting area to the orthopedic office unseen. Which is to say that we are not here because we consider you a suspect."

Idell entered with a blue-lacquered tray containing a teapot and three cups and saucers, a bowl of sugar cubes, small bowl with a couple of lemon wedges, and a small pitcher of cream. All the dishes were fine china. There were tongs for the sugar and spoons of very heavy stainless to stir with.

Idell set the tray on the coffee table and looked her question at Cal, who said, "One lump is great."

The maid dropped a cube into Cal's cup, poured, set a spoon on her saucer, and handed her cup. She repeated this for Patty, with two lumps of sugar rather than one, then looked a question at Mason. When he shook his head no, Idell withdrew, leaving the tray.

"I wish I could say I'm relieved," Patty said. She sipped her tea. "But since I couldn't have killed Ms Sauer . . . ?"

Cal said, "Why are we here?"

Patty nodded.

"Video surveillance showed that you were one of the last people to leave the building. We were wondering whether you might have seen something or someone you didn't expect to see."

Patty took a moment to consider this. "I ... There was someone behind me as I left the building that I didn't recognize. A man, roughly your size ... no, a little shorter, wearing a blue windbreaker with a yellow ... a gold design. I barely noticed him, since I was trying to get to the assembly point to check in."

Cal nodded, and Mason asked, "Are you aware that Marlene Sauer was telling people that she was engaged to your husband?"

Patty set her cup on the table and folded her hands.

She's keeping her hands from shaking, Mason thought.

"I had heard she was engaged," Patty said, "I never heard a particular name associated with her fiancé."

"May I ask," Cal said, "Since you are obviously wealthy, why are you working as a nurse?"

Patty paused, seeming to consider the intent of the question. "When I was a senior in high school and Walter was in college, he was running a small business. He probably had thirty employees. I became his bookkeeper — everything was computerized, so I really just did data entry. Walter ... went through all the young women working for him. Fortunately for him, I had turned eighteen by the time my father found out. That kept Walter out of jail, but not off a marriage license.

"I went to nursing school and became an RN after Walter and I were married. We both worked hard, and he started more than one business that became profitable, and then was sold to some larger company. After the second such sale, I quit working as we planned to move here. This house is more ostentatious than I intended — that was Walter's doing.

"When I had enough of his serial adultery, I told him I was bored and wanted to go back to work. But my real plan was to accumulate enough independent cash so I could afford better lawyers than his and come out very well in the divorce settlement. The kind of lawyers I wanted don't take divorce cases on spec."

Mason contemplated this for a moment and said, "I have spoken with your husband. He indicated that you … encouraged him to move out."

Patty's hands were trembling now.

"The latest woman, Ms Sauer, as you told me, was too much. He missed social engagements *he* set up. He missed at least one business dinner, leaving *me* to represent his business when he was with *her*. That was the end. I wasn't waiting any longer. I could pay the lawyers out of what I made in divorce. So I packed his bags and left them on the front porch. And had the locks changed."

Cal nodded. "Good for you," she whispered.

Mason and Cal thanked Patty for her time and extracted themselves from the house. As Idell showed them to the front door, Mason caught Cal's eye and nodded toward Idell.

Cal thanked Idell for the tea and asked her, "Is there a chance you and I could sit down and talk this afternoon or sometime tomorrow?"

"I would be happy to this afternoon," Idell said. "Could we meet for coffee, say, or a smoothie?"

Cal said, "A smoothie would be good. I've been told

Mrs Stancill will be at work this afternoon. Could we meet midafternoon — say, around three?"

"Three o'clock will work for me."

Idell suggested a place, then the detectives departed.

Driving back to the road, Mason said, "Sorry to spring that on you."

"It's not a problem for me — I'll get a smoothie and be happy. But why do you want me to meet with Idell?"

"Because we need corroboration for what Patty just told us and for what Walter told me the other night. And I'm convinced Patty knew that Walter's latest conquest was Marlene Sauer."

"I thought so, too," Cal said. "Do you think Idell will be able to confirm that?"

They waved at the gate guard as they exited the uncommon Commons.

"Probably not. Walter may be arrogant, and he may have slipped up, but he's not so stupid as to have brought Marlene home with him."

1:35 p.m.

When the school clinic called Ron to say Ed was not feeling well, Clarissa Penfield — she smiled just saying that to herself — went to pick him up while Ron called and arranged for the doctor to see him. Now she and Ed were on their way from the school to the Booker Medical Building.

"I know you're not happy about my being here," Clarissa said.

"It doesn't matter," Ed muttered, staring out the window.

"Nothing matters."

Clarissa was pretty sure she knew what was eating him.

"You wish your mom were here."

"But *you* don't. You're too busy being ooey-gooey with Dad."

"Look, I know this all happened suddenly." Ron and Clarissa's first date had just been four months earlier. "But you need to know that I miss your mom, too. For months, she was my only friend."

"If she was here, you wouldn't take her place."

Now it was out in the open.

"I'm not taking her place," Clarissa said.

"Right. You sit with us at church, and you fix dinner in Mom's kitchen, and you're even in Dad's *bed.* You're *taking her place.*"

Clarissa took a couple of slow breaths.

"No one but Barbara Penfield could be your mom. I get that. And you need to know that I sort of understand."

"Right." Ed's voice was full of doubt.

"After my dad walked," Clarissa said, "my mom had men in. At different times a couple of them moved in. When the last one tried to pick me up, she threw him out and hasn't had anyone since. She even started buying her own beer."

"That's pretty messed up." His gaze moved from the terrain outside his window to the glove compartment door directly in front of him.

"And before, I didn't even *know* it was messed up. Except for that last guy — I knew that was bad."

She went on, answering his points. "And yes, I'm your dad's wife," — she had to smile again, despite the tension in the car

— "and yes, I believe what your dad believes, as much as I understand, and there's so much to learn. But I'm not half the cook your mom was. I've just about shot the wad on the special things I cook."

Ed's gaze moved to the steering wheel in front of Clarissa. "The food has been good so far."

They were parking in front of the doctor's office.

"I just hope I can keep it up."

1:48 p.m.

"I am sorry you had to wait sir." Lilia Argyros was answering the phone at the front desk of the General Practice office at Booker Medical Building. The receptionist, Cheree Ohrt, had asked her to pick up after the caller started swearing at her.

"I don't mind waiting a reasonable amount of time," the man shouted in a gruff voice Cheree could hear. "But that thrice-damned on-hold music is terrible. I'd rather have plain silence."

"I will pass that on to the communications staff. They have not spent much time on hold themselves."

"Well," the man was calming down, "perhaps that's a good idea. Now —" he went on to describe what he needed. Lilia wrote it all down and promised someone would call with confirmation.

"I love your voice," the man said, completely calm now. "It … never mind."

They rang off, and Cheree said, "Crisis averted?"

Lilia nodded and went back to the nurses' station in the

center of the practice. She found the information the patient had needed and dispatched an assistant to call the patient back, then went back to the reception desk.

A woman and a young teenage boy were talking with Cheree.

"This is Edward Penfield," the woman said, "and I'm the wicked stepmother."

"We're expecting you," Cheree said. "Have a seat and someone will see you in a few minutes."

"Excuse me," Lilia said across the desk. The boy went to sit down, but the young woman turned back. "Are you the new Mrs Ron Penfield?"

The woman smiled, "Yes, I am. Do you know Ron?"

Lilia said, "Yes, we met when he worked with my ex-husband, John Mason."

"The detective? What a small world!"

"Suffocating," Cheree said under her breath. There wasn't much room at the reception desk.

Lilia took the hint and held up a forefinger, meaning *wait a minute.* She stepped back around and out the patient entrance door.

"I am so glad to meet you. I am Lilia. Lilia Argyros. I met . . ." She stopped, realizing she was about to mention Barbara.

"I'm Clarissa. Clarissa Penfield." She smiled again — she couldn't help it. But she understood what Lilia was about to say. "Barbara was a friend. We all miss her very much." She indicated the youngest Penfield. "Ed and I were just talking about that."

"I will not keep you," Lilia said. "But we will take care of Edward." And with that she disappeared back through the entry door.

Back at the reception desk, she saw that Clarissa and Edward had taken the closest seat to the desk. Edward had buried his nose in a book.

"Now, Cheree," Lilia said, "I hate to do it, but we need to call a staff meeting for tomorrow morning. Just a brief one, for, say, seven forty-five. I want *everyone* there. No exceptions. When the alarm sounded on Monday, I went back through the halls, checked doors. I know — I am *certain* that the tag was on the restroom door in the back hallway, but I was coming back through after checking everything and someone *came out of that restroom.*"

"*After* it had been checked?"

"After. Definitely after."

A nurse passed them, opened the entry door, and called, "Edward Penfield?"

Lilia saw Clarissa and Edward stand and follow the nurse, Patty Stancill, back toward the exam rooms. Lilia said "I will be here around seven tomorrow to work on scheduling while there is no one in the office to interrupt. It would be a favor if you would come by and make sure I'm at the meeting on time."

Cheree assented, and Lilia went back to her office.

3:00 p.m.

Cal entered Smoothie As Glass promptly at three p.m. and saw Idell Hendricks waiting at a table.

"Have you ordered?" Cal asked.

"Not yet. I thought it best to order together."

Cal nodded and they walked to the cashier. As Idell went

first, ordering a smoothie heavy in fruit and yogurt, Cal looked around.

She had expected something like an ice cream parlor — light colors, pastels, big letters. But this was more upscale than that. What she saw instead was more like a cozy meeting place, like a Starbucks maybe. Cal wouldn't have been surprised to see a committee of soccer moms gathered around a table. She did see a couple of people working on their computers and talking on their phones through Bluetooth headsets.

When it was her turn, Cal ordered a high-protein smoothie suffused with raw grains and dark berries.

"You didn't need to do that," Cal protested when Idell paid.

"It's all right. Stuck in the big house with a four-person staff and employers who work — employer now, I guess — I don't have much social life. I'm just happy to share a few minutes with someone. Sooo . . . "

"So, why are we here?"

Idell nodded and took the first sip of her drink.

"We are looking for independent confirmation of some of the details of what Walter Stancill told Detective Mason."

"And," Idell said, "to be complete, of what Mrs Stancill told you this morning."

"Just so." Cal took a sip of her drink. It was delicious; she'd need to remember this place.

"First, why Mr Stancill?"

"You heard about the killing at the clinic where Mrs Stancill worked?"

Idell nodded.

"The victim, Marlene Sauer, was telling people she was engaged to him. Had he ever gone so far as to be engaged to someone he was sharing a liaison with before?"

"Not that I know about. Walter — he's out of the house, so I'll use his first name. Walter would work long hours, and when he found a girlfriend for a while, he would 'play' for long hours as well. As the housekeeper, I heard a lot of arguments between them, but this was the first time Mrs Stancill made him leave."

"Do you think Mrs Stancill knew who his latest conquest was?"

"I'm certain she knew."

"How can you be sure?"

"Because she got me to follow Walter when he left work one day — it must have been two or three weeks ago. It was the evening after a business dinner at the house where Mrs Stancill had to entertain two of his clients solo. Just as they were leaving, Walter came in disheveled. The next evening, at Mrs Stancill's direction, I followed him as he left work and drove to an apartment, and I saw him embracing a woman in the entrance. I didn't take any pictures, but I gave her description to Mrs S."

Cal swallowed and said, "Just have to ask: Did you get paid extra for doing that?"

Idell swallowed in turn and said, "I already get paid half again what other Arcadia housekeepers get. That was at Mrs Stancill's insistence."

"Was there ... an occasion for this ... insistence?"

"Walter made advances toward me."

"You were able to repel him?"

"I told him I'm gay. It's partly true." She looked at Cal from beneath an arched eyebrow as she sipped her drink.

Cal blinked in recognition. But only recognition. "I'm spoken for," she said.

Idell nodded acknowledgement.

"Do you think Patricia knew Marlene Sauer's name?"

"It's easy enough to find with just an address and an online search."

Cal finished the thought. "And then confirm she works in the same building you do."

Idell sipped her drink down to halfway. "I don't know about that. But Mrs S was ... utterly bitchy until Sunday night."

"Really? This past Sunday?"

Idell set her cup down. "Yes." She paused. "Look, I don't want to give this gig up: I have an MA in hospitality, but I'm making way more than I would be by now in the hotel business. And I made it sound like I'm lonely before, but I have a lot of freedom within the bounds of my job."

"This," Cal said, "is something I understand."

They finished their smoothies chatting about music and movies and books. Cal returned to the station, and Idell went to complete her afternoon household business.

4:07 p.m.

"What's the verdict?" Ron asked as Clarissa and Ed entered the kitchen from the garage.

"Ear infection," Ed said.

"Not contagious," Clarissa said, "so he's okay for school tomorrow as long as he gets plenty of rest."

Ed headed up the back stairs to go to his room.

Clarissa looked at the clock. "I'd better get to work on supper."

"Nothing doing."

"Is there a problem?" Clarissa was suddenly unsure of herself.

"No!" Ron said, "It's just that we have a lot of leftovers, which have been great, including some that Gloria left here when we got home. We need to eat what we have."

"Okay." Clarissa was relieved. "Oh! I met someone at the doctor's office you know, a Lily Archerose I think."

"Lilia Ar-JEER-ose, yes; she was John Mason's first wife."

"She's drop-dead gorgeous! I bet people go to the doctor with fake complaints just to get a glimpse."

"She's beautiful, certainly."

"So why did they divorce?"

Ron explained about how Mason had become a workaholic because he couldn't handle having an autistic daughter.

"But," he concluded, "he has been seeing their daughter, Adena, regularly since last summer. John told me they're getting along pretty well."

"Hmm."

"What?"

"Seems like something-holics are a running theme right now." Clarissa took a quick breath. "I was thinking, since Ron has moved out, why don't we offer his room to Ed as long as he's in town?"

Ron wasn't *quite* gobsmacked, but he did pause. "Umm. He would be here during the day . . ." he said slowly.

"And there's only one more day before Saturday," Clarissa reminded him, "when Ed and Lenna will be home anyhow. And his room is the farthest from ours."

Ron couldn't move, almost couldn't breathe for half a minute.

"I hate to admit it, but you're right. I'll call to invite him."

"And invite him to supper. He's family. He can have leftovers like the rest of us Penfields." A smile forced itself to her lips once again.

When Ron could breathe again, he called Ed to invite him.

"Tell you what," Ed said. "Checkout time was few hours ago, so I've already paid for tonight. How about I bring my stuff over tomorrow around lunchtime?"

"Sounds great. Leftovers tonight?"

"I'll be there. What time?"

Ron told him, and when he rang off, he told Clarissa.

4:25 p.m.

"So now we have Patricia Stancill lying about knowing her husband had moved in with Marlene Sauer," Cal said after she relayed the contents of her conversation with Idell.

"Almost," Mason said. "She knew they were seeing each other, and it's safe to think she would presume they still were. If she knew he moved in, that would be icing on the motive cake. But the cake is the point, not the icing." He took a drink of water.

"And still no opportunity."

"Still no opportunity," Mason echoed. "Anything else?"

"Nothing bearing on the case. We talked movies and books while we finished our drinks."

Cal's desk phone rang. She answered and listened.

When she rang off, she said, "We have financials on Edward Penfield. Who's on first?"

Mason bit his lip to keep from making the joke. "You go ahead. Write down what you observe. I'll go through it all in the morning, then we'll compare notes."

Cal nodded and turned to her computer.

Mason started shuffling through the papers, interviews, labs, everything, but not looking at anything, just trying to get everything to fit into place. Nothing was cooperating.

5:02 p.m.

When nothing came together in all the reports, Mason turned to his computer. He found an email from Lukas Sauer. Lukas would arrive at the Atlanta airport late Friday afternoon, and he had reservations for a rental car and a hotel.

Mason decided it was time to talk to Walter Stancill again. As the original presumed next of kin, he needed to know that Lukas would be coming in, and he would probably want access to Marlene's apartment.

He placed the call to Walter's office and was put on hold. He waited for ten minutes, then hung up and called again.

"Hi, yeah, this is Detective Mason with the Bristow Police. I was cut off from my call to Mr Stancill. Can we be reconnected?"

The receptionist complied, and Mason found himself talking to an irritated Walter Stancill.

"How did you get through?" Walter demanded.

"It doesn't matter," Mason said firmly. "You and I have to talk, and this is official business."

"And it couldn't wait?"

"Even if it could, I don't care. I have new information that *you* need, and I'm going to tell it to you now."

Stancill growled, "What's so bloody important?"

"I'm glad you asked," Mason said with the barest sarcasm. "Did you know that Marlene had a brother?"

"She may have mentioned him once. I'm not sure. Why?"

"He is her legal next of kin as named in her will, and he is coming to town. He has a hotel room and a car, but I'm sure he will want to go through Marlene's apartment. That's in addition to taking possession of her body."

"Do you know what his plans are for Marlene's funeral?"

"No idea," Mason said.

"I suppose I should move out of the apartment."

"I think that's best. Just to remind you: Please don't take anything out that you didn't bring when you moved in. This case is proving difficult, and I need to be able to look for clues in Marlene's belongings."

"I understand. Is that all?"

"One more thing: We'll need your contact info, and I'll send Detective Caligari to pick up your key to the apartment. That's all for now."

"Very well," Walter said, and he rang off quickly.

"Detective," Cal said as Mason hung up his receiver.

"Hmm."

"Did you know you make more hand motions when you're on the phone than when you are talking with someone in person?"

Friday, November 9

7:40 a.m.

At seven forty Friday morning, Cheree, the receptionist at the general practice office, checked Lilia Argyros's office, and, not finding her, wound her way back to the storage closet where Lilia kept her espresso machine.

Lilia was tamping espresso grounds into the filter basket.

"Sorry to interrupt," Charee said, "but we need to start the meeting in a couple of minutes."

Lilia nodded and grimaced. She'd have to come back to make her espresso. It wasn't real Greek coffee, but it was the best she could do in the office.

Almost all the staff of the practice was gathered at the nurses' station, the only open area big enough for everyone at once, when Lilia arrived. A couple of folks approached from a different direction.

"Everyone is here. Very good," Lilia said. By Lilia's fiat even the doctors were present.

"This is a safety briefing," Lilia said.

Someone standing behind everyone, whispered, "I thought those were held at O'Malley's." A couple of people snickered. Lilia went on.

"The reason we are meeting is that someone did not follow emergency protocol on Monday. I don't know who, and I am not asking for anyone to confess. This is what happened: A door tag was hung on a room, I believe it was a restroom, and when doing my room checks, I passed by it, thinking it had been cleared. But when I was on the way to exit the building, *someone came out of that room.*"

Someone asked, "Was anyone missing from the roll call outside?"

"No, there was no problem with that. But if someone, a patient or even one of us, were disabled and in a room with a door tag, the result could be tragic."

Everyone looked around at each other.

"That's all. These protocols are in place to make sure everyone is safe. If no one has anything else, let's get to work."

The crowd dispersed to the places they would be when the office door opened at eight o'clock.

Lilia wound her way through the halls to her espresso machine's hideout, through a hallway narrowed by filing cabinets hugging a wall, two doors past anywhere any patient would go. She would have done this as planned at seven o'clock, but Mrs Vaughn, who usually drove Adena to school on Fridays, was late arriving that morning.

In the small room, a storage closet, she engaged in a ritual known only to her coworkers.

She finally initiated the mechanism that would give her a mug of coffee as close to Greek as she could get on a workday. She threw the switch, and the espresso machine began heating water.

Lilia waited patiently as pressure built up in the steel chamber, until the water she had put in earlier was pressurized enough to force its way through the dark, fine grounds. She filled her mug with enough for a double espresso, probably a little more. Adena had painted the mug for her all those years ago, while Lilia and John were still married. It was a medium indigo, the color of slightly faded jeans, with dark indigo around the rim and the inside. She smiled thinking of her daughter, and with the passing of the years, she was no longer bitter thinking about her ex-husband.

Detaching the basket/spout, Lilia dumped the grounds into a wastebasket just outside the door and went to her own office. She drank her espresso and worked for about forty-five minutes on staffing schedules covering the next month, accommodating vacations and other requested time off the best she could. Her stomach began feeling odd. Surely, she wasn't becoming ill. As for normal symptoms, the timing was off.

Her abdominal distress grew more severe. She grabbed her cell phone and headed for the restroom — the same restroom she had heard someone exit on Monday. Her cramping was not relieved by her diarrhea. She punched the direct number for the nurses' station. Someone answered.

"This is Lilia. I am violently ill, in the restroom in the back hall." She tried and failed to keep the contents of her stomach from sloshing onto the floor. When she could catch her breath, she said. "Doctor. Emergency."

Less than a minute later, a doctor and two nurses came through the door. "Diarrhea, cramping, vomiting," she said.

The doctor looked amazed, frightened, and alarmed, all at once.

"Oh my God!" he whispered. Louder, "Do we have any dimercaprol?" One nurse understood and ran to the dispensary, shouting at the pharmacology nurse. When she returned, the doctor prepared the injection and administered it and waited until, without looking back at the staff crowded around the restroom door, he said, "Someone call the police. She's dead."

8:50 a.m.

One of the nurses went to tell Cheree Ohrt to block the door and lower the rolling door to the reception desk. Locking the door was illegal, but Cheree's substantial size would provide an effective barrier. Cheree held her cell phone as she stood in front of the door, and from it she first called nine-one-one, then called the building security guard.

The guard arrived first, got a look at the scene, and ran to the practice's other restroom where he lost his breakfast. He came back, pale and panting.

Two patrol officers arrived, and immediately surveyed the scene. One had a white blob under his nose. The other said "Can I have a hit of that?" and the first passed him the little jar of Vick's, which he applied to match his partner's. They sent everyone who had not been in the restroom back to their normal standby locations.

A second police unit arrived, and one of the officers took Cheree's place at the office entry while the other waited at the building entrance for detectives, CSU, and medical examiner. They arrived in that order.

The detectives were Mason and Caligari.

Seeing Lilia on the floor like that, Mason told Cal to call Lieutenant Tejeda and ask that Michael Renfroe be shaken loose from whatever he was doing and dispatched to Booker Medical Building, pronto. Then he went to an empty exam room and wept silently.

The CSU team that came in behind the detectives went about their tasks sullenly, collecting the samples they had to have. They knew that Lilia was Mason's ex-wife.

When Mason returned, red-eyed, he said, "You instructed them not to talk to each other, yes?"

Cal nodded.

He left one officer making sure the CSU team was unhindered.

He called the remaining officers and briefed them and Cal and Michael Renfroe, who came in just as he was starting. "Start interviews. Get the morning routine, what everyone did and everywhere they went since arriving. You know the drill. I want to talk to anyone, *anyone* who said more than good morning to her."

They all assented and went off to get started.

All except Renfroe. "You okay, John?"

"No. I am not the hell okay. I have a daughter who's now motherless."

"Should I call Sergio and get someone else to lead on this?"

Mason shook his head *no*. "You're the lead; Cal's secondary; I'm third. If you think I'm not helpful, then tell me and call Sergio on your own judgement."

Renfroe nodded understanding and went off to start interviews.

Mason poked around in the rooms nearest the restroom and found what he expected: Nothing.

9:16 a.m.

Cal returned with Cheree Ohrt to the exam room Mason was using as field headquarters. "You remember Ms Ohrt, Detective?"

Mason nodded.

To Cheree, Cal said, "Tell Detective Mason what you told me about this morning."

Cheree seemed nervous. "We all liked Lilia," she said. "She was great at her job and she cared and she could calm someone who was angry and . . ."

"I understand," Mason said. "Was that what you needed to tell me?"

Cheree said, "Sorry — I'm nervous. I babble when I'm nervous. Anyway, we had a staff meeting this morning, an extra one."

"What was it about?"

"Well, Monday, during the evacuation, Lilia said someone didn't follow the protocol, so she called the meeting this morning to make sure everyone was briefed."

"Were there any objections? Did anyone raise a ruckus?"

"No, everyone understood."

"What did Ms Argyros do after the meeting?"

"I didn't see her myself. But I'm sure she went to make herself a cup of expresso." Mason didn't bother to correct her. "She was getting ready to make it when I interrupted her to come to the meeting. She had her expresso machine in a back room, a storage room the staff knows about but the patients don't. She made it in the cute mug she said her daughter made."

"And she didn't make it before the meeting?"

"No, sir. I had to interrupt her to start the meeting."

"Can you show me her office?"

Cheree nodded and started walking away.

"Hold on," Mason said, and gathered a CSU tech to go with them.

On their way to the back, Mason asked, "She didn't make the espresso in her office?"

"No. I don't think she wanted to. I think she wanted a hideaway, kind of."

Lilia's office was locked, but Cheree had a key.

"She kept the office locked," Cheree said as she opened the door, "because she had personnel records and other confidential papers in here."

Cheree stood aside as Mason looked through the door. There was a desk covered with papers, file cabinets against one wall, a small bookshelf against another wall.

But Mason only saw one thing: the mug Adena had made all those years ago.

"Are you all right, Mr Mason?" Cheree asked.

A lone tear rolled down Mason's face. "Just thinking about Adena."

"You knew Lilia and Adena?"

"Lilia is ... was ... my ex-wife. Adena is my daughter."

A couple of moments and a couple of deep breaths later, Mason entered Lilia's office. He set his emotions aside. Most of them, anyway.

"Work schedules," he said looking at the papers. "We can leave those. But the coffee cup still has a little in it." To the tech, he said, "Take possession of the cup — we have to test the contents."

Turning to Cheree, Mason asked, "Would Lilia have had anything to eat, or just the coffee?"

"I don't know, sorry."

Mason looked around. He was done in here. "Take me to the room she kept her espresso machine in."

The tech sealed up the mug, but before he left, Mason told him, "Come find me or send one of your team when you drop that off."

Cheree led him around multiple turns, past file cabinets in a narrow hallway that dead-ended with a door on the left. Indicating the door, she said, "It's in there. This door is never locked."

Mason nodded, put on gloves, and opened the door, which opened in and to the left on a storage closet that was about six feet by eight. Gray metal shelves lined the walls, stocked with boxes and gallon bottles; a clipboard hung from a vertical support on the corner of a unit. The only place that had no shelves was in the back right corner, where a small table stood, with just enough room around it to make access easy. On the table stood a home espresso machine.

He told Cheree, "Go back to the intersection and flag down the CSU tech that comes looking for us."

The tech arrived and Mason told her, "Take possession of the espresso machine; contents to be tested. I want a full workup on this room: prints, dust, compare the contents to the inventory on that clipboard, note any bottle or box that has been opened. And the trash can just outside the door, that too."

The tech nodded and got to work.

10:08 a.m.

A few of the staff were brought to Mason for a second interview. In each case, the detective or officer who brought someone to talk to the detective stayed, but the officer remained silent and did not prompt. Later Mason would find out whether the same story was told both times.

The one interview in which Mason went beyond what the officer had heard was Dr Jensen, who had administered medication to Lilia just before she died.

"So why did you administer . . ."

"Dimercaprol." The doctor filled in.

"What did you suspect?"

"I did a couple of years as an ER doctor in South Georgia," the doctor said, "and a residency in toxicology. I had a couple of cases of arsenic poisoning from farm chemicals. A supervisor was not using the stuff according to the very specific directions."

"Violating federal law."

Dr Jensen nodded. "Exactly. Those cases were long, slow exposure, but I knew the symptoms of sudden large doses and sort of intuited what Lilia had probably ingested."

"In your opinion, was this likely to be someone trying to kill Ms Argyros on purpose, or might it have been an accident?"

"Without other evidence?"

Mason nodded.

"I don't want there to be enough of the killer left to bury."

3:00 p.m.

"I don't like it." Mason said as he drove Cal and Refroe back to the station. Renfroe had come to Booker Medical Building with a patrol car, figuring Mason would want to talk on the way back. "Two murders in the building."

"In different offices," Cal pointed out from the passenger seat.

"By very different methods," Renfroe pointed out from the back seat behind Cal.

Mason halted the car at a four-way-stop intersection.

Cal: "One was where no one could have done it."

Renfroe: "The other was where anyone could have done it."

Cal: "One was a nurse."

Renfroe: "The other was an office manager who was working on staff schedules."

Cal: "The nurse was leaving her job because of a hostile work environment and a rich fiancé."

Renfroe: "The office manager had habits known by everyone in the office. More than half of the interviews mentioned the espresso machine."

Cal: "Except for a few who insisted on saying '*ex*presso'."

Cal (again): "For the nurse, the only person with opportunity was not medically trained, but the killing was so precise, there's no way to hit that artery by dumb luck."

Renfroe: "For the office manager —" He interrupted himself. "Sorry, John — damn. I know it's hard for you."

They were still stopped at the stop sign, and had been through the whole exchange. Mason finally looked at the traffic and drove on.

"Sorry," he said. "I have to go tell my daughter that her mother is dead."

They proceeded in silence the rest of the way back to the station. Mason pulled up to the curb in front.

"Cal, I want you to do a deep dive into Ed Penfield's past. See if he ever worked as a hospital orderly, paramedic, anything like that, maybe that's how he worked his way through law school. Also, I need a summary of his financials. I'll be late getting to the office tomorrow, so you have time for a thorough sweep.

"Michael, go through all of today's witness statements and develop a timeline of ... Lilia's ... movements since she got to work. Get the ME's office to check for arsenic first, then everything else. Get verbals from forensics on body fluids. There were ... plenty ... of those."

Even though both had been given instructions, neither moved.

They sat like that for a couple of minutes.

"Boss," Renfroe said quietly, "you need to park and get someone to drive you where you need to go."

Mason nodded. The younger detectives got out, and Mason drove to the staff lot and parked.

He pulled his cell phone from his jacket pocket, looked for a number in his contacts. He found the one he wanted and tapped to call.

The voice at the other end was surprised and friendly. "Hi, John. What's up?"

"Ron, I need a favor."

4:25 p.m.

"Daddy, did something happen to Mommy?"

Adena had expected her mother to come home.

"Adena, there's no easy ... way ..."

John choked up and couldn't talk.

Adena sat quietly, looking at her kitchen table knothole.

"Your mother ... died today."

John had called Mrs Vaughn and told her already. She now sat at the table across from him.

Adena's mouth tensed.

"How did she die? Was there an accident?"

This keeps getting harder, John thought. "Someone poisoned your mother." He anticipated her next question. "On purpose."

They sat for several minutes.

"Will I be staying here?"

"That's up to you, Adena. You may choose. If you stay here, Mrs Vaughn will stay with you."

Mrs Vaughn nodded. "That's right," she said softly.

"Or if you want, you may come home to my house."

"Will Ann be there?"

"Yes."

"And tomorrow?"

"If you stay here, I will come by in the morning and take you to my house. If you don't want to go to there, Mrs Vaughn will stay with you here. If you do come to my house, I will bring you back here in the morning if you want."

"I will help as much as I can," Mrs Vaughn said.

Adena stared at her knothole some more.

"I will . . . May I come with you?"

"Absolutely. Yes. Mrs Vaughn will help you pack."

While Adena packed, John called Ann to tell her Adena would be at their house tonight.

Ron Penfield had waited in the car for them for over half an hour. John and Adena sat in the back seat; John wondered whether he should try to hold his daughter's hand.

As they drove toward John's house, no one spoke. John felt awkward in the silence, but he had learned over the months that Adena didn't mind it.

John's phone rang. Lukas Sauer was calling to tell him he had arrived at the Atlanta airport, and he would be heading to one of the hotels Mason had recommended. He had purchased a cell phone and gave Mason the number. Mason thanked him, and they rang off.

"Was that about the woman who was killed on Monday?" Adena asked.

"Yes."

"In Mommy's building?"

"Yes. It was the woman's brother. He just arrived from Germany."

"Is this the nurse who was engaged to Walter?"

"Your mother told you about that?"

"Yes, sir. Walter used to visit Mommy."

John's head twirled to face his daughter. "Wait. You know Walter?"

"Yes, sir."

"Walter Stancill?"

"Yes, sir."

John got his phone out and placed the call.

"What, John?" Cal sounded out of breath. John could hear weights being lifted in the background.

"Walter Stancill is connected to both murders."

"Should I bring him in?"

"Not yet. But in the morning, get with Michael. You need to work out timelines for different scenarios."

"Will do," Cal said, regaining her breath a little.

At John and Ann's house, Ann welcomed Adena. Ron waited in the car as John took the girl's luggage into the house.

After maybe five minutes, John came back, and Ron drove him to pick up his car.

Ron said, "Ed should have left a message for you by now. He's moved out of the hotel and into my house and is staying in Ron Jr's room starting tonight."

John nodded acknowledgement.

"I know you shouldn't talk about the Sauer case with me, especially since I'm related to one of your suspects."

"Right. So we won't talk about it."

"Okay. Tell me about Lilia."

"Someone poisoned her espresso. Forensics says it was arsenic."

"Was Walter … Walter Whatever in the building? For either killing?"

"No. But he's connected to both — you already heard me tell Cal that — so we have to figure out what the connection is."

"If there is one," Ron said.

They rounded the last corner to John's parking lot entrance. The entrance was blocked by a lift gate, so Ron stopped outside it to let John out.

"I hate to make you rat on your own brother, but if he says anything related to the case, can you let me know?"

"Sure. He didn't kill Ms Sauer, so I'll pass along anything that he says."

"I don't think he did either," John said. *But I can't find anyone else with opportunity*, he thought. "Thanks for the lift."

Saturday, November 10

7:15 a.m.

Saturday morning saw John and Ann up early, trying to figure out who would take care of Adena and when.

Ann had appointments with clients starting at noon, and they were going to take her into the early evening. She guessed she would be home by six or seven.

John needed all the time he could get for working two homicides, but he understood that he wasn't the only person around. He reflected, silently, that after Adena's diagnosis, he had withdrawn from her and her mother. He pushed the bitterness and sadness and regret and guilt feelings down. He would have to find time for those later.

What they finally worked out was that John would go to work after Adena woke and had breakfast; Ann would work from home for the morning, at least until Mrs Vaughn could get there.

Just as Adena wandered into the kitchen studying the grain of the wood floor, Mrs Vaughn called John on his cell phone.

She could be there by ten o'clock.

John prepared breakfast for Adena (two scrambled eggs and toast) and himself (two eggs over easy, toast, and grits). Ann had eaten a protein breakfast bar, so she sat and drank her coffee while father and daughter ate.

As they ate, Adena asked, "Are you in charge of the investigation of Mommy's death?"

"No, but I'm helping with it."

"Please do your best."

John felt tears welling and his nostrils clogging when she said that. When he could talk again, he said, "I promise."

When they finished eating, John put their dishes in the dishwasher, then went to his bathroom to brush his teeth. When he returned to the kitchen, he sat at the table again with Adena.

He said, "I know you're not much for hugs, but may I hold your hand for a minute before I leave?"

Adena nodded and put her hand almost halfway across the distance between them. John took her hand gently, just for a minute, then released it and said, "Goodbye, Adena."

"Goodbye, Daddy."

John motioned for Ann to step into the garage with him. They hugged.

John said, "Thanks for doing this."

"You're my husband. Thank *you* for arranging Mrs Vaughn so I have time to work, too."

He nodded, then they hugged again, then Ann went back into the house as John got into his car.

9:53 a.m.

Mason met Lukas Sauer in the tiny lobby of his hotel. Lukas was of average height, slender, with wavy brown hair and a thin mustache that ran past the ends of his mouth. His eyes were brown and small, and he wore a heather-blue sweater and gray slacks.

"I hope your room is all right," Mason said.

"Yes, it is very comfortable. What do we need to do today?"

"Let's sit down."

The men did so in armchairs stuffed into either side a lobby corner. "First, we will go to the police station for some paperwork that will begin the process of releasing Marlene's body to you. We will not be able to release her body until the Medical Examiner's office has completed all its work, but we will have the paperwork ready for that time."

"Will I be allowed to see Marlene's body?"

"If you wish."

Mason noticed that the hotel had a complimentary coffee urn on a table in another corner. "Can I get you some coffee?"

Lukas's expression soured. "No, thank you."

Doesn't like American coffee, I guess. Mason dispensed coffee for himself. "While we are seeing to the paperwork, I'll arrange for you to see her body." He covered the paper cup with a lid.

"Is there any question of how Marlene died?"

"No question." Mason resumed his seat. "She was poisoned with a common chemical used to clean medical equipment. It was injected into her neck when she was alone in the office."

"How could she have been alone? Was the office closed?"

"No, it was early morning, and the practice had been seeing patients for a few minutes. Someone tripped the fire alarm. Marlene was in charge of making sure everyone was out of the office."

"Was the fire set deliberately?"

Mason nodded. "Yes." After explaining, he stood. "Let's go to the police station."

"What should I bring?"

"Just your passport will be fine."

Lukas assented and rose. Mason led him to his car and drove them to the station.

As they drove, Lukas commented that about half the trees were in glorious autumn colors. Then he asked, "Do you know whether Marlene had made final arrangements ... no ... *funeral* arrangements for herself?"

Mason turned a corner. "We have her personal papers, including her will, but I don't believe there is anything about her ... final disposition."

"Will you be able to help me find a ... crematorium? Is that the right word?"

"It is the right word. There is one near the police station, and others will be easy to find if that one is not to your liking."

At the stop sign that had given him so much trouble the night before, Mason asked, "Were you in regular communication with Marlene?"

"Not as regular, perhaps, as we should have been. I was aware that she was seeing someone. Can you tell me about him?"

"Yes. I have spoken with him. He is a local businessman. He had left his wife and moved in with Marlene. They were planning to be married following his divorce." Mason finally drove on from the stop sign.

"I am sorry to bother you with so many questions. But will I be able to meet this ... boyfriend?"

"I can call and ask whether he is willing," Mason said. "Certainly, the police have no objection."

"And is her former husband, Edward Penfield, aware of her death?"

"Yes. He still lives in Mississippi, but he is in town now." Mason debated with himself whether to say more about Ed Penfield, but he decided it should wait.

Mason turned into the police station parking lot, found a space, and parked. The two men went inside and back to the detectives' bullpen. Cal was there, going through stacks of paper.

"Hi, John," she said. "I didn't expect you this early."

"Detective Caligari, this is Lukas Sauer."

Cal rose and offered Lukas a hand, and met his eyes. "I am so sorry for your loss," she said.

"*Danke* ... umm ... Thank you," Lukas said, his gaze fixed on Cal's eyes.

Cal broke her gaze away from Lukas's and started to tell Mason about her research on Ed Penfield, but Mason stopped her with a hand motion.

"Can you check with the M.E.," Mason asked Cal, "to arrange a look at Marlene's body this morning?"

Cal nodded and sat to make the phone call.

Mason made a copy of Lukas's passport and prepared paperwork for the transfer of Marlene's remains.

Cal had told Mason about the appointment the M.E. had given for the viewing of Marlene's body at the morgue. The two men left to perform that sad, grisly duty. Afterward, Mason took Lukas back to his hotel.

Then he went to catch up with Michael Renfroe's progress.

11:00 a.m.

Renfroe had read most of the statements from people in the general practice, and he had a timeline of Lilia Argyros's movements roughed out on a sheet of paper. He handed it to Mason without saying anything. It was titled, *Movements, Lilia Argyros.*

- 7:35 arrived at office, told receptionist to send everyone to the nurses' station as they arrived
- 7:37 restroom
- 7:39 seen in the back hallway where the espresso machine was
- 7:43 nurses' station
- 7:45 staff meeting
- 7:52 seen in back hallway again
- 7:58 in the hallway with coffee mug headed toward her own office
- 8:00 entered her office.
- 8:45 seen hurrying to restroom
- 8:47 phone call to nurses' station
- 8:49 doctor arrives
- 8:51 doctor injects her with dimercaprol
- 8:53 doctor declares her dead

"M.E.?" Mason asked.

"Definitely arsenic. Powder, added to the grounds of her espresso. Dry grounds were found in the trash can outside, presumably to make room for the powder. Also, wet grounds from the cup she made. Her coffee was pretty strong — she wouldn't have known it was there."

"Arsenic is tasteless anyway. But she would complain — always, I mean, not just yesterday — about how weak espresso was."

Renfroe went wide-eyed at that.

"You've never had Greek coffee, have you?"

"Had some Turkish coffee once. Just once."

"They are essentially the same thing." Mason made a weird hand gesture, but Renfroe didn't ask.

Mason started going down the list in his mind. "Prints?"

"None."

"Just like with Marlene. In a medical office, you can wear gloves ..."

"... and no one will notice," Renfroe finished.

"Inventory?"

"The clipboard in the storeroom was the inventory list for the supplies in that room; there's another, larger storeroom with the same setup. Everything lined up exactly in both. Boxes had been opened, but none of the containers *in* the boxes had. And neither had any of the bottles."

"A well-run practice. Lilia would have seen to that." Mason squeezed his lips between his teeth for a minute. "How aboooout ... Do any of the chemicals stored in the office — *anywhere* in the office contain arsenic?"

Renfroe put the question on his list.

"Was the front door locked?" Mason asked.

"To the building, no. It opens at six-thirty. The receptionist, Cheree, doesn't let patients into the practice until eight when they open, and she says she was the first one there at a couple of minutes after seven. But the rolling door over the receptionist's desk was raised just before the staff meeting."

"Rats. Anyone with clean shoes could get in and out without being noticed. Did you get camera footage from the waiting area?"

"Got it; haven't reviewed it."

"Do that next, start at six-thirty and go to half an hour past time of death. It should show everyone who entered. Cheree and Lilia would have had their own keys. Talk to Lilia's assistant and find out who else had them."

Renfroe added it to his list.

"The office had been open for almost an hour," Mason said, "Are any of the statements from patients?"

"Yes, there were half a dozen patients inside the practice at time of death. A few more had come through before. Only one saw the victim, and that was when she was hurrying to the restroom."

A plain-clothes officer approached Michael's desk with a bag and a receipt. He looked at the receipt and paid him.

"Get the list and start calling whoever had been there that we didn't talk to. Get whatever help you need. Also, I want to talk to Walter Stancill here."

"Is this the right case? I mean, shouldn't Caligari have that one?"

"I learned last night that Stancill used to be Lilia's boyfriend."

"Umm, is that a good idea then, Coach? You talking with him?"

Mason sighed. "Probably not. You and Cal will talk to him together. We'll talk strategy when you have a time set up. And let Cal know —"

"I heard," Cal said from across the room. "Let me know what time, Michael."

"*Today*," Mason said.

Renfroe added it to the top of his list, where he had left room for high-priority items.

Mason walked back to Cal's desk.

"Tell me about Ed Penfield."

Cal got the summary notes where she had written them down. "Okaaay. Ed is heavily in debt."

"How deep?"

She told him, and he whistled.

"*But* six months ago, it was worse. There used to be multiple charges per week at a liquor store. It built up over years."

Mason held up a finger. "Ed told me he has been sober for six months and a few days."

Cal nodded. "He started making payments to a rehab center five months ago."

"When you talk with him, ask if he spent that month in rehab. The answer will be yes. What else?"

"This is a little harder to follow, but his alimony payments were trailing off, getting smaller and smaller until he went into rehab, and they stopped while he was there. But then when he got out, they went higher than the steady state they had been in before they started getting smaller."

"Presumably to make up for what he had missed." Mason headed toward the break room. "Hold on a minute." He returned a few minutes later with a cup of coffee.

"Fresh coffee," he said so everyone working could hear it. A couple of folks headed that direction, though neither Cal nor Renfroe did.

"Okay," Mason said to Cal, "how about anything medical in

Ed's background?"

Cal thumbed through her notes. "He worked as a hospital orderly after college for a year before starting law school, and then for his first two years of law school. He and Marlene got married, and she supported them for his third year."

"A little thin for medical knowledge," Mason decided. "Was Marlene already an RN when they met, or did he maybe help her prepare for ... whatever the certification thing for nurses is?"

" 'Boards,' I think," Cal said. "She passed those right before they got married, so he may have helped her prep for it."

"Sooo ... he moves a notch back up the scale."

"It would be ironic if he helped her learn what he later needed to know to kill her."

"It would be," Mason said, sipping his coffee, "though motive is still pretty low on the scale."

"Does that count?" Cal asked. "We really only need means and opportunity. The latter he has in spades, but the former? We searched him *and* his car and found nothing."

"He was straightening out his life, he was paying off his debts, including to Marlene."

"So if he wanted to pay off other debts faster ...?"

"We'll put that in the 'not rejected' pile. But we'll hold it until we've eliminated everything else. And you and Michael need to share everything on Walter Stancill." He spoke across the room. "You got that Michael?"

"Yes," Michael said through a mouth full of cheap taco.

"I'll be back after a while," Mason said to Cal. "Can I bring you back some lunch?"

"No thanks," she said, "I'm doing my normal thing."

"You must be holding yourself pretty strictly to a training

regimen. How serious is this volleyball thing?"

"Everyone needs a hobby, John. Something you're willing to sacrifice for. Jeri and I won't be in the Olympics, but we may win a city or regional amateur event."

Mason reflected on his own past. "But if your work becomes your hobby, it can cost you a great deal." He almost whispered as he said, "At one time, it cost me my family." *And now is Adena my hobby?* he thought. *Or is she my new work?* He was leaving the room as his face twisted momentarily in grief.

11:00 a.m.

Ed had come to the Penfield house on Friday around noon, and today he had pried Ron away from Clarissa for lunch. When they returned, Ron set him up for work in his home office, which was directly under the bedroom Ed was staying in.

The first Saturday breakfast since the newlyweds had returned from their honeymoon took all morning. Ron and Clarissa prepared bacon and pancakes. Young Ed (as they were calling Bumper temporarily) grouched his way to the kitchen, his surliness softening as he ate. Ed joined the family for breakfast, and he and Lenna had chopped pecans in their pancakes. When Young Ed saw he could do that, he asked for another serving. And when they were about halfway through the second round, Ron Jr came in and was instantly hungry when he smelled bacon, so the bell rang for round three. Coffee, orange juice, and milk flowed freely.

By the time everyone was done, even Young Ed was laughing and trading stories about things that had happened through the last three weeks.

When everything was cleared and the dishwasher was running, Ed and Ron sat at the table with fresh coffee.

"So you were driving Detective Mason around last night," Ed said. "What's with that?"

"If you look at the news, you'll see that there was another killing at the Booker Medical Building yesterday."

"And?"

Ron said, "The victim was John's first wife. When they were married, they had a daughter. Last night, John was … not distraught … distracted? that will do … distracted by the prospect of how he now has to raise her without her mother."

"Did he say anything about Marlene's case?"

"He found out something that —" Ron cut himself off. *Should I tell Ed this?* He took a minute to decide. "Sorry, Ed, can't tell you."

"Don't apologize. I understand confidentiality. So is there a plan for today?"

Ron picked up the entertainment section of the newspaper. "I was going to take anyone who wanted to go to the movie to see that animated animal comedy. Tell you what: Will you take a poll and see whether anyone is interested?"

"Sure, why not?" Ed got to his feet and searched out everyone while Ron washed the pancake griddle in the sink.

When Ed returned, he said, "Young Ed, Lenna, and your lovely wife all said yes. Ronny — sorry, Ron Jr — said he has to get to campus for baseball practice. He thinks they may redshirt him in January. In the athletic sense, not the *Star Trek* sense."

Ron grinned. "Yeah." His eyebrows lowered. "I did remember something I can tell you: Marlene's brother is in town."

"Lukas? Hmm. We only met a couple of times, at the wedding, and then when we went to Leipzig before Cory was born. I guess he's here to take care of all the estate stuff." He took a deep breath and exhaled. "I guess I should apologize to him, too."

12:30 p.m.

As he left the detectives' squad room, Mason placed a call.

"Hey, John," Ron Penfield said. Mason could hear laughter in the background. "Are you doing better?"

"Yes, thanks. I was hoping to buy you lunch."

Mason heard a deep breath being drawn.

Ron said, "I can't eat anything — I'm too overstuffed from breakfast. But I can get a drink and maybe steal a fry or two. Where do you want to meet?"

Mason named a place and said, "Fifteen minutes?"

And fifteen minutes later they were sipping drinks and shelling peanuts while Mason waited for his burger. Ron was sitting at an angle to the table, so by turning his head one way he could look out the glass storefront and turn it the other way to look at his friend.

"I just wanted to warn you that it's not looking good for Ed on Marlene's murder."

"Explain," Ron said.

Mason did so, telling Ron about how the murder was committed, how Ed was the last person known to see Marlene Sauer alive, how he was among the last to exit the building, how they had learned Ed plausibly had sufficient anatomical knowledge to have targeted the right spot on Marlene's neck.

Mason's number was called for his food, and he met someone who was bringing his bag to him.

He sat back down and extracted his burger from the bag. The fries were in a large cup, which he dumped out on the bag so they could share.

Mason took the first bite of his too-big burger as Ron picked up a fry and twirled it in his finger.

Ron ate his fry and said, "Extra napkins," and got up to get them.

When Ron returned, Mason said, "Thanks, I always forget."

Ron ate another fry, and then he observed, "So you have opportunity in spades. And knowledge of means, but nothing to actually link Ed to having possession of means. What do you have for motive?"

Mason swallowed. "Look, I can't give you my whole case. I'm here as a favor to a friend to say that I *may* have to arrest your brother if a prosecutor thinks there's a case." He took a sip of his drink.

Ron sipped his own drink.

Mason said, "So how is everyone getting along with the newlyweds?"

"Everything is fine. Clarissa and Lenna are becoming fast friends. Ed the Younger has had the hardest time adjusting, but he and Clarissa have something like a truce going, sort of a *détente* or *rapprochement.* A peace treaty is imminent. Ron Jr has moved out to a house he and friends are renting. I told you that Ed came to stay at the house, right?"

Mason nodded and chewed.

"Ed's staying in Ron's room, and he gets along great with everyone — he's the 'cool uncle.' Bumper is named after him."

"I guessed," Mason said between bites. "How about Gloria?"

"She has been in Houston since we got back — we crossed paths in the airport as we were arriving and she was leaving. Ron dropped her off and picked us up."

"How did she feel about her grandkids' father marrying someone who wasn't her daughter?"

Ron snorted and smiled. "I think she would have set us up if I hadn't asked Clarissa out on my own."

"And how was the Caribbean?"

"It was great. Completely relaxed. We found a little waterfront bar with good food half a mile from our hotel, and we walked to it three or four times."

Ron took a sip of his drink and grimaced.

"Something wrong?" Mason asked.

"No, we had pancakes this morning and this is just too sweet after all that."

"When I finish this, want to hit the GNW?"

"Sure ..." Ron wasn't sure what was up, but he knew Mason needed to talk. "I need to be home by two o'clock. I'm taking everyone to a movie."

They talked about the college football season as Mason finished his lunch.

"I need to wash up," Mason said, rising.

"Tell me what you want at the Great Northwest. I'll go ahead and order, and it will be ready when you get there."

Mason told him, then headed to the restroom while Ron drove on to the coffee shop.

1:06 p.m.

Their coffee orders were ready just as Mason walked in. He found a seat in the corner, the same seats Ron and Ed had occupied on Wednesday, while Ron picked up their drinks. The house music was pop hits arranged for two classical guitars.

As they settled into their seats, Ron said, "So what's up, John?"

Mason sipped his drink. "I don't know whether you've seen the news yesterday or today . . . "

"Haven't gotten to it yet. What have I missed?"

"Lilia died yesterday."

Ron set his drink on the table in the corner between them. He clasped his hands over the arm of his chair. "Oh, no . . . How? Was Adena hurt?"

Mason breathed heavily to keep from crying. When he had control again, he said, "Adena is fine. Lilia was killed at work."

" 'Was killed.' On purpose?"

Mason nodded.

"*Murdered.*"

Mason nodded again and took a hit of his coffee, sitting in the solace of a friend's silence for a few minutes.

Mason looked at his coffee and chortled at the irony. "Someone, some . . . some *person* put poison in her espresso machine at work."

After a minute, Ron asked, "What about Adena? Do you need help caring for her?"

"We're okay for that. The lady who helps with Adena after school is with her at our house." Mason took a couple of sips of his coffee. "Adena's going to have to move in with me and

Ann. But our hours are so strange, and Adena needs order in her life — it's how she deals with things — and our lives are so ... 'chaotic' is too strong. Varied, at least."

"Whatever we can do," Ron said, "any time you need it."

"Will you be going back to work on Monday?"

Ron swallowed a sip of coffee. "Yes, both of us. But we can —"

Mason held up a hand to cut him off. "Thanks, I'll remember it. But here's something you don't know: Lilia worked in the same building as Marlene Sauer."

"Actually, I did know. Our family GP works in Lilia's practice. Clarissa took Bumper there on Thursday. But are you working the case?"

"I've got Michael Renfroe doing the leg work, and I'm watching over him. I told him that if I get out of line, he can tell our captain and get me kicked off."

"Is there any chance the cases are related?" Ron asked. "Two poisonings in the same building in the same week."

"I don't like coincidences. But these have too much *not* in common: Different method, different practice. And they were in two different parts of the building with no communicating doors.

"If the same person did both killings and works in the building, they'd have to cross the waiting area — that's the only way to get from the GP office to the orthopedic office, and the video from Monday doesn't show anyone crossing between those offices or anything like that. I'll know about yesterday, about ... Lilia ... anyone crossing ... I'll know about that later today."

Mason's phone rang.

"Mason. ... Okay, I'm headed back now. Start brainstorming and we'll give it some shape when I'm there. Should be ten minutes."

They both stood.

Ron said, "I know you don't believe, but Clarissa and I will be praying for you anyway."

"Couldn't hurt. Thanks."

1:45 p.m.

At the station, Renfroe looked up as Mason walked in. Cal was sitting across the desk from Renfroe, who asked, "We have about forty-five minutes. So how are we going to do this?"

"Is Walter bringing a lawyer?"

"He asked, but I said this was just a chat to gather information away from the distractions of his office. I hinted we wanted to know more about his wife."

"That's good," Mason said, nodding.

"It was Cal's idea."

"Also," Cal said, "we traced his alibis for both murders, and for both he was at his office five miles away. Which brings me to this: Why are we talking to him, again?"

"Fair question. We're talking to him, not because he committed the murders, not because we *think* he committed them, but because he's *connected* to them. He may have hired someone to do them, but we won't find out about that today. But he may tell us something *he* thinks is irrelevant but it has a bearing on one case or the other." To their quizzical looks, he added, "No, I don't know what."

"So where do we start?" Renfroe asked.

"We start by making sure he knows Lilia Argyros is dead, was killed at work, that we knew he used to be involved with her, and that we're hoping what I said before: he may know something that connects the two killings *besides him.* Tell him we know he wasn't in the building, he's not a suspect. It'll be three o'clock, so ... what do we offer him as a snack?"

"Anything in the machine," Renfroe said. "Nuts, chips, candy bar."

"I've got a protein bar," Cal added.

"And I'll put on fresh coffee," Mason said. "Okay, break for now, and both of you meet him in the lobby. Or talk some more now, I don't care. But if you have any brilliant ideas before he gets here, let's talk together."

The younger detectives nodded and went to continue looking through papers.

Mason called Mrs Vaughn to ask how Adena was doing. When she picked up, he could hear the piano in the background, playing a classical piece he wasn't familiar with.

"She seems quieter than usual. I'm not surprised, really, and I am only a little worried."

"I understand. I'm worried, too." *About more than I can tell you.*

"Has she been working on any school at all?"

"She started on math, but she was having trouble concentrating and put that aside. She started playing the piano more than an hour ago and hasn't gotten up from the bench since."

This was a whole new world for Mason. "What do you recommend?"

"I'll give her a few minutes more, then I'll interrupt her the standard way."

"The standard way?"

"We have a set of 'how to interrupt Adena' things to do," Mrs Vaughn said. "I suppose I should write them down for you."

"That would be tremendous help — that and any other everyday knowledge. I have been learning bits about it over the last few months, but I know there's a lot more. Anyway, I should be home by six o'clock. Or is that too late for you?"

"Six will be fine."

Mason thanked her and rang off.

1:45 p.m.

"Met a friend for lunch and coffee," Ron said, as he drove to the movie theater.

"It's the second meal we've had apart in three weeks," Clarissa added, slightly wistful.

Ed asked, "How could you possibly eat anything after breakfast? And as I recall, you ate twice," he said, pointing at Ron's stomach. "Unless you had worked up quite the appetite —"

"Didn't eat," Ron cut in. "Had about four of John's fries and tried to drink a Coke, which I couldn't finish because it was too sweet after all that syrup and honey."

"John?" Ed asked. "Mason? Did he want to talk about me?"

Ron realized he had slipped. But he had started, and he had to go on.

"Partly."

"Sooo ... what is happening with the investigation? Are they any closer to knowing who killed Marlene?"

"I don't think so. But ..."

Without anyone seeing, Young Ed had taken out his earbuds. Lenna still wore hers.

"I don't know how much I should say." Ron silently recriminated himself for the slip. "It doesn't look good for you right now, Ed."

"How bad is it?"

Ron breathed heavily for a couple of minutes, carrying the burden of decision. "I can't ... discuss particulars. You appreciate that."

Ed nodded.

"But he's looking into your life, and a lot of things are piling up that make it ... plausible that you did the deed."

"The good news is I didn't."

"I know," Ron said quickly. "But an overzealous prosecutor who gets hold of a case like this may be able to convince a jury —"

"Stop right there," Clarissa said. "The cases we hear about — the false capital convictions — are really very few and very far between. There are too many, yes, any is too many, but the news likes to make lots of noise about them because it gets eyeballs to watch their commercials."

"I hope you're right," Ron said.

"I hope we don't get far enough to find out," Ed said.

Young Ed said, "You could always run for it," he said. "Might be fun."

Ed and Clarissa looked at him and Ron glanced at him in the mirror; all three wondered how much he had heard.

"Running would only make my case worse," Ed said. "I'd have better chances on the street of a big city where no one knows me. There are plenty of those. Movies make it look more possible than it is in reality. But I don't have any illusions about my chances of making it. Besides, I ran away for too many years, drinking. I'm not running away from this."

Ron and Clarissa breathed quiet relief.

"You said my case was partly what he wanted. What else was there?"

"Have you seen the news about the other killing in the same building?"

Ed and Clarissa both nodded. They had traded sections of the paper after cleaning up the kitchen.

Clarissa suddenly realized what she had read. "It was that Lily woman with the Greek name."

"Lilia Argyros," Ron confirmed.

"Wait," Clarissa said. "Didn't you tell me she was John Mason's ex-wife?"

"Yep."

"Who?" Bumper asked.

"The tall, beautiful woman we saw talking to the receptionist at the doctor's office," Clarissa said.

Ron drove the car into the theater parking lot.

"Wait," Ed said in turn. "Didn't I see her in the lobby, waiting to talk to the police on Monday? After Marlene died?"

"That's the one," Ron said. "John wanted to talk about the burden of raising their daughter. How hard it will be for a cop and a real estate broker, two people with weird hours, to raise a high-functioning autistic teenager."

"Wait!" Bumper said, "Adena is autistic?"

"Yes."

Bumper's forehead creased and he was staring at the curb as they crossed the parking lot.

To Ed, Ron said, "Speaking of things you've run away from,

why don't you come to church with us in the a.m.?"

Ed gnawed on his lip for a minute. "I suppose I have to."

"No, you don't" Ron said, smiling. "It's not like that. We're going, and you're welcome, that's all."

"Then ... I suppose I should. Several steps in the program mention God."

"I know. But there's a weakness, a problem with your steps."

"Problem? I thought you'd be pleased. How can there be a problem?"

"The problem is that it's not a specific god they talk about. They'd be happy with Zeus or Odin or Buddha — I know, the Buddha's not a god, but you get the idea. It's some general, vague notion of a 'god' that functions as an instrumentality — a means to an end. It's 'God As I Imagine Him,' not God as he revealed himself in Christ and the Bible. There's a God who's really *there*, not as my servant, but as 'my Maker, Defender, Redeemer, and Friend.' "

Ed was astonished. And his eye glistened at the words he hadn't heard in almost twenty-five years. "Maker ... Defender ..."

"Look at it this way," Ron said. "When a soldier is wounded on the battlefield, the medics get him off the field, patch him up enough to get him to the doctor. But if all he ever sees are the medics, he stays wounded. Your program corresponds to the medics. You should be grateful *to* the medics and grateful *for* the medics. But your real need is the surgeon."

The old Ron had been a regular churchgoer, but this was almost someone different. "How did you get here? To believe that, I mean?"

"Do you remember — no, you wouldn't. There was a time

a few years ago when Barb kicked me out; it was after Dad's funeral. We were in trouble because I was working so hard on becoming a counselor that I wasn't home when I was home."

"I had no idea."

"The best thing I could do for a few weeks was to stay out of Barbara's way, so I started going to a small church, Trinity Reformed, where we go now. Instead of tips for living, I heard about sin and forgiveness, not like a revival preacher, but like — well, like a surgeon. I got Barb to come once when our old church was being so shallow your toes wouldn't get wet, and we've been going there ever since."

Ed said, "I haven't seen anything like that. I think I need to go." *And if it's a cult,* he thought, *I'll have to figure out how to get them out of it.*

Clarissa glanced at the clock on the dashboard. "We need to go inside," she said. "Anyone want to take odds on whether we'll want popcorn?"

3:00 p.m.

"We really appreciate your coming in," Cal said as she and Renfroe met Walter Stancill in the reception room of the station.

"We only got to talk for a minute when you came to get Marlene's papers," Walter said. "I hope my coming in means you're making progress on her case."

"We are making progress. This is Detective Michael Renfroe."

The two men shook hands. "Come on this way to the conference room," Renfroe said.

"The room with the two-way mirror?" Stancill asked.

"No," Cal grinned. "That's for suspects. We just want to see if you have some information that can help us decide whether someone is telling us the truth."

"Whatever I can do to help."

They reached the conference room, and by careful maneuvering the detectives got Stancill to sit where the camera Mason was using to observe had a three-quarter view of his face but was out of his line of sight.

"So, what can I help you with?" Stancill asked as he sat.

"Well," Cal said, "when I picked up Ms Sauer's papers the other night, you said you were planning to move out, so first we need an update on where you're living."

"Sure. I got a weekly, furnished apartment with decent internet." He gave the address and apartment number, which Renfroe wrote down. "As soon as I can find a better place, I'm going to get some furniture and move. I still have the other detective's card — Mazing? No, Mason. I'll leave him a message."

"Sounds great," Cal said. "Here's one of mine. Michael, will you give him one of yours?" As Stancill was pocketing their business cards, she told him, "Feel free to call any of us with anything you think of that may be relevant."

Stancill nodded acknowledgment and waited.

Renfroe asked, "I presume you keep up with the news?"

Stancill nodded again.

"Then you know that Lilia Argyros was killed yesterday."

Stancill nodded yet again, cautiously this time. "I suppose," he said, "you somehow found out that Lilia and I were involved a while back. Since we broke up, I haven't seen her even a handful of times. The last time was months, maybe even a year ago."

He had a look that said, *Do I want to call my lawyer now?*

His face was so easy to read that Cal said, "What? Oh, no. No, no, no! We don't suspect you in either death. To be honest, we talked with your secretary, and we know that you were nowhere near the scene of either death."

Stancill looked visibly relieved. "Then I have to ask again: What can I do for you?"

Cal said, "Well, we don't like coincidences here, and outside the vicitms' workplace — meaning both Ms Sauer and Ms Argyros — you are about the only thing we can find that the two deaths have in common."

Stancill muttered something under his breath.

"What was that?" Renfroe asked.

"I said, 'If you don't count how angry Patty was.' She was genuinely fit-to-be-tied angry. She almost threw me out when Lilia and I were involved until I broke it off. But she didn't give me that chance with Marlene. I presume she has leashed some lawyers by now. And she's smart enough that they will be good. Very good."

Cal made her face look curious. "Why did you break up with Lilia? She was beautiful and completely poised. I interviewed her Monday, and frankly, I was impressed by her, maybe even jealous."

"I originally told Lilia that I would marry her. I knew she had a daughter, Athena. No. Adena, that was it. And I was okay with that. But when I found out she was partially autistic — that's not the official terminology, but you know what I mean — I knew she would take extra attention."

"And money, presumably," Renfroe said.

"I didn't care about the money. Making money is easy. It

was what I said; it was about the *time*. Adena was a sweet kid, but I wasn't going to be able to devote any real time to her, to help Lilia. Can you tell me what's going to happen to her?"

"I believe she is living with her father," Renfroe said.

"I hope he takes good care of her, can give her the extra attention she needs."

5:00 p.m.

As John walked into his kitchen, he saw Adena sitting at the table with Mrs Vaughn.

"Hello, ladies!"

Mrs Vaughn nodded.

Adena said, "Hello, Daddy." Her eyes scanned over the surface of the table, looking for something.

"Is everything okay?"

Mrs Vaughn said, "Adena is looking for her spot on the table."

Adena corrected her. "This is not Mommy's table. I can't find a place to focus."

"Perhaps," John said, "If you move to a different chair, the difference in perspective will help."

As Adena was moving to a different chair, Mrs Vaughn said, "Dinner is warming in the oven; salad is in the refrigerator. I had to make a trip to the store; I left the receipt by the refrigerator. If it's all right, I need to go now."

John said okay, and the caretaker was off to her evening.

After a couple of minutes, Adena sighed with relief. She had found her spot.

John said, "Adena, tell me about your day."

Adena said, "After you and Ann left, I tried to work on schoolwork, but I was unable to concentrate. I kept trying and ... couldn't. After a while, Mrs Vaughn suggested that I play the piano. So I did. You have a nice piano."

"Having a piano was Ann's idea. What did you play?"

"*The Well-Tempered Clavier*, Book One and Book Two. It took three hours, seventeen minutes."

"That's a long time. Did you take a break during all that?"

"Yes. Mrs Vaughn suggested it, so I took a break between Book One and Book Two."

"That makes sense."

Without a hint of bragging, Adena said, "I know."

Adena thought for a minute, then said, "Your piano needs to be tuned."

"I'm sure you're right. Ann has not been able to play much for a long time. I will arrange on Monday for someone to tune it as soon as we can."

Just then Ann came in and said, "Something smells wonderful! Hello, dear. Hello Adena."

Adena returned Ann's hello without looking up, and John stood to hug his wife.

"Have you been home long enough to cook?" Ann asked.

"No, Mrs Vaughn made dinner. It's in the oven."

Ann asked, "Adena, did Mrs Vaughn cook for you often?"

"She would cook for me and Mommy twice each week, on the days Mommy had to work later."

Adena drew her knees up and rested her chin on them, wrapping her arms around her legs.

Ann asked "Sweetie, are you okay?" and crossed the room to put her hand on Adena's shoulder.

Adena shrugged Ann's hand off, and sat quietly, concentrating on her newfound spot.

Ann came back to John with a question on her face.

He whispered, "Probably having to think about her mother."

Ann nodded and asked, "How do I apologize?"

"No idea. Right now, let's serve dinner. I'll wash up after."

Ann went to the oven and removed the big cast iron Dutch oven. John got the salad from the refrigerator and plates from the cupboard. He set the table with flatware and napkins as Ann portioned out the roast beef, potatoes, onions, and carrots from the pot onto plates. She added salad from the bowl to each plate while John sliced Italian bread from the loaf.

As Ann got red wine from the rack and began pouring for herself and John, John set Ann's and Adena's plates on the table, and asked his daughter what she would like to drink with dinner.

Adena whispered, "Ice water," so John got a glass and dispensed ice and water from the refrigerator.

They sat and ate. John told Adena she only had to eat as much as she wanted, and if she wanted more, she could have it.

Ann said, "Tell me about your day, dear."

"I watched as Cal and Michael talked with Marlene's fiancé, hoping to learn more about her to help us discover suspects. Right now, we don't have any."

"And the financé is not one?"

John shook his head. "No. He was miles away from both scenes."

"So you're treating both incidents as having one perpetrator."

"Not exactly. While it may be a single perp, the dissimilarities are sufficient to at least hold the possibility open. Had lunch with Ron Penfield. Told him about . . . " His eyes darted to his daughter and back to Ann.

Ann said, "Adena, what did you do today?"

Adena repeated word for word what she had told John.

John asked Ann, "And your day?"

"I'm this close," she held up thumb and forefinger about an inch apart, "to a big sale."

"How big?"

"About fourteen mill."

"Sooo . . . A million commission?"

Ann nodded as she chewed her final forkful of potato.

When they had finished dinner, Ann put food away as John began loading the dishwasher. Adena carried dishes from the table for John without being asked.

When dishwasher was running, John asked Adena, "Would you like to watch TV? We can watch anything you like."

"No, thank you. May I play the piano instead?"

"Sure. May I listen while you play?"

"I would like to listen, too," Ann said.

"Yes. That is fine."

Adena sat on the piano bench in the living room and began playing. John wasn't a musician, but he could tell there was a complex interplay of . . . he wanted to say "voices," but did that make sense?

Ann whispered, "That is one of the most complex, chromatic fugues in the *WTC*. And she is not stumbling over any of it."

After a few seconds, she said, "We should get that tuned."

When Adena had finished after two preludes and fugues,

John and Ann both complemented Adena on her playing, and she received their comments with reserved grace.

Her mother taught her well, John thought.

"I'm going to bed now," Adena announced.

As Ann went to change into pajamas, John locked up and reflected that his family suddenly had a new — very, very new — normal.

Sunday, November 11

7:47 a.m.

On the way to the sports complex, Constance Wall asked Michael Renfroe, "So what is it we are going to watch?"

"Amateur league beach volleyball."

"And why?"

"Because we need to get out more," Michael said, "and because my semi-partner is half of a two-woman team."

Constance wasn't convinced. "There can't be that many people who play that. I never heard of it before you suggested we go."

When they exited onto the half-mile-long ramp from I-285 to I-75 north and Michael was pretty sure no one was going to hit them merging, he said, "This is an Olympic sport. And I think you'll like Cal."

" 'Cal'?"

"Catherine Caligari. You met her last summer at John's Fourth of July picnic."

"Okay, well, I'll watch, once. After that, we'll see. But what does 'semi-partner' mean?"

"John is leading investigations into the two murders at the medical building. I'm nominally the lead on the second murder and Cal is assisting on both."

"Oh, the two nurses, and both are immigrants."

"Almost right. One was a nurse, the other an office administrator." They merged into traffic on I-75 proper. "Both were naturalized citizens, one from Germany, the other from Greece. John and Cal were working the first case when the second happened. I was called in because the second victim was John's ex-wife. I'm working that case while Cal ping-pongs between the two. Because the murders were in the same building, we have some overlap."

"His ex-wife?" Constance spat out. "You mean the tall woman from the picnic last summer?"

"That's the one."

"The one who wore a *white skirt* to a *barbeque*?"

Michael nodded.

"And left with it *clean*?"

"Yep."

"And *she* was murdered?"

Michael nodded again. "So because John had a history with her, he brought me in to make sure he kept to the path."

"And this Cal person . . . "

"Like I said, you met her at the picnic: Kind of tall, athletic build, brown hair."

Michael ccouldn't see Constance's eyebrows narrowing. "The one who was edging up to you until I hung myself on your arm?"

"That's the one. Then she went off and spent a lot of time

talking to that short teenager. And in the football game, she was the one who stuffed the perp's mouth with the rag."

Constance spoke quickly. "I hate to sound jealous, but why did you notice her talking to a young girl?"

"Because that *particular* teenager was involved in a case from last year, the one where your Mr Penfield's wife was killed."

Constance retracted her emotional claws.

And extended them again when she saw that the female players were in two-piece swimsuits. But when the wind kicked in on that sunny, chilly November Sunday, all the players covered up with T-shirts or muscle shirts, and Michael was safe again. Relatively.

The matches alternated between women's and men's games, with games going simultaneously on two adjacent courts in single elimination matches.

Cal and her teammate, Jeri Strickland, won two games, but lost in the semifinals. They came over to say hello and meet Constance.

When she saw them approaching, Constance grabbed Michael's arm and hung on. *To be fair*, Michael thought, *she is shivering.*

Cal and Jeri had pulled on matching sweatsuits and sneakers. They were breathing hard, and Cal said, "Can we walk and talk? Need to cool down."

Jeri was an inch or so taller than Cal, had a straighter nose, and wore her blond hair short.

Everyone agreed, and they walked a path that made a circuit around the volleyball part of the complex.

Talk turned to other hobbies. Michael mentioned kayaking on the reservoirs, and how he had taken Constance with him.

Cal was quiet during this, but Jeri mentioned needlework, and Constance said, "Really? What type do you do?"

"I do freehand embroidery. And my grandmother taught me tatting."

Constance stared at Jeri. "Handmade lace?"

"Yeah," Jeri panted. "It's not as common as knitting, but it's pretty interesting."

"Do you do any work for other people?" Constance asked, "Professionally, I mean?"

"Some," Jeri said, "as a sideline. I did embroidery on a dress, a caftan, for a woman to wear as she left for her honeymoon. It was a little hard to see because the colors were so close, but it came out fine."

"A 'caftan'?" Michael asked.

"I'll explain later," Constance said. "It has embroidery around the neck and sleeves. Wait ..." She looked at Jeri again. "It wasn't the Penfield wedding, was it — Clarissa Penfield?"

"That's the one," Jerri said, smiling, "How did you know?"

"We were at the wedding," Constance said, holding Michael's hand tighter. "I work with Ron Penfield. That dress was gorgeous."

"Thanks," Jeri said as humbly as her panting allowed.

They finished a third circuit of the volleyball center and said goodbye. Cal and Jeri went to watch the women's final, and Constance and Michael headed toward the parking lot.

"That was more fun than I thought it would be," Constance said as Michael opened the car door for her. "Now get me something hot to drink."

9:04 a.m.

As Michael and Constance were exiting I-285 onto I-75, John and Ann were talking over a quiet breakfast. Adena came in dressed neatly in a skirt and blouse, hair brushed, and makeup applied with a light touch.

"You look nice," John said.

"Thank you."

"What would you like for breakfast?"

"Scrambled eggs and toast if that is all right."

John rose and fetched the small frying pan from the dishwasher. He prepared Adena's breakfast, then sat quietly with her as she ate. Ann went off to change for her morning run.

When Adena had finished eating, John said to her, "What would you like to do today?"

"Mommy has been taking me to church in Marietta."

That explains her being more dressed up. "Why did she go all the way to Marietta?"

"That was the closest Greek Orthodox church."

John nodded. Lilia had seldom attended church when they were married, but 'seldom' isn't 'never,' and of course she would return to the kind of church she had known growing up.

"I don't know how Orthodox churches are scheduled," John said. "Did you only go on Sunday?"

"Sometimes we would go to Vespers on Wednesday, and then Mommy would stay for confession."

John took a minute to absorb this. Here was a change in his life he hadn't thought of. Doctor's visits, school conferences, maybe some activities if Adena had any; he had expected these.

But church? *New normal*, he thought. "What time does the service start?"

"Divine Liturgy begins at ten a.m."

John calculated drive time to the Marietta Square, and asked, "Will you be ready to leave in ten minutes?"

"Yes, Daddy."

"Then we will go." John stood and turned to go to his room to change. But he turned back to ask, "First, though, how do most men dress for this meeting?"

"Many dress in coat and tie; some in slacks and dress shirt."

Adena rose and took her dishes to the sink, then turned toward the other kitchen exit.

"All right," John said, "Go finish whatever you need to do."

Just then Ann came back into the kitchen, dressed in a lightweight jogging suit and running shoes. "Where are y'all headed?"

John drew a breath, "We're going to the Greek Orthodox church in Marietta."

Ann clenched her lips between her teeth for a moment.

"It's part of the new normal," John said.

John departed the kitchen by one exit; Adena, by the other; Ann by the door to the garage to stretch before her run.

9:15 a.m.

As the Penfields were piling into the minivan to go to church, Patty Stancill was leaving her mainline church, where she had gone to the early service. She had reasoned, correctly, that Walter would go to the eleven o'clock service to be seen, because Religion Is Good For Business.

She, for one, didn't intend to let his departure ruin her life. It would be an inconvenience, like the change into and out of Daylight Savings Time. Like the time change, Walter was a Necessary Evil. And now this Necessary Evil would be starved of the affection (ahem) that he seemed to live for. And her lawyers would see to it that he was relieved of a sizable portion of his other great love: money.

Patty had stood and sat and recited and sung and pretended to listen like just about everyone else. Eventually, the decaying hold religion had on the South would rot away, but until then, Patty wouldn't allow events to interrupt her peace.

She wouldn't have to worry any more about Walter's serial adultery. Perhaps he would persuade someone he bedded to marry him, so he could continue his adultery (if nothing else). It was time someone else paid. Patty simply wouldn't.

She turned on 128 to head to the gym for practice. Her gymnastics coach held open hours from eight till noon on Sunday, so if not too many showed up, Patty could get some extra time with her, beyond the two evenings when she was in the group sessions. She was one of her instructor's best, keeping her weight down, unlike the other women about her age in the class.

Balance beam today, she thought with a wry grin.

As she was stretching and warming up, Patty decided that today was not gymnastics day, but meditation day. She couldn't help wondering what (or who) Walter was doing today. So she apologized to her coach and headed to her yoga studio for the eleven-thirty class.

10:55 a.m.

Walter Stancill, as he was driving to church, wondered whether he would run into Patty. He caught a glance at her car (recognizing the tag number) as he turned into the parking lot just after she had left. He wondered whether she had seen him. Then he wondered whether he cared. Then he wondered whether *she* cared.

He had bought a new suit this week — getting thrown out of your house meant going without some of your old stuff — and he had to admit that he looked very good, very business-like. He shook hands with other business owners who attended, who in turn introduced to him one or two new men who would probably be in the circle soon.

When the service started, he stood and sat and recited and sang, and during the sermon he missed Marlene. He supposed he really would have married her after Patty had wrung him and raked him and mauled him, financially.

When the service was over, he was shaking hands with more of his peers. One asked about Patty, and he answered that they were newly separated.

When he finally left, he followed a friend who was also recently separated, to a chain restaurant, and they commiserated about their ill-tempered spouses as they ate Caesar salads with grilled chicken.

Monday, November 12

7:15 a.m.

Ann was just sitting at her kitchen table with her second cup of coffee and her newspaper when Adena entered.

"Adena, why are you dressed for school?" Ann asked.

"I should go." Adena said.

"But sweetie, no one expects you to go now, not for a few days, anyway. Maybe next week. Mrs Vaughn is on her way over to stay with you today."

"I should go to school," Adena repeated. There was no more emphasis in her flat voice, no body language to suggest she was insisting.

But Ann was at a loss.

John came into the kitchen, and he immediately sensed Ann was troubled.

"What's the problem?" he asked.

"Adena wants to go to school."

John went to his daughter and said, "Let's sit down."

They sat, Adena where she could see her spot on the table, hands resting in front of her; John next to her.

"May I hold your hand?"

Adena nodded and left her hands where they were. John reached out to gently hold one.

"When something tragic happens, people need time to mourn. And you may be extraordinary, but you are a person, and you need time to mourn."

Adena did not respond.

"Will you stay here with Mrs Vaughn today?"

"If I must."

"*Should* you stay?"

Adena hesitated, eyes never veering from her spot.

"I . . . do not . . . think so."

John's mind was such a scrambled mess for a couple of minutes, that he could only get shallow breaths.

Finally, he took and released a deep breath. *A new normal.*

"You have my phone number," he said at last. "If anything makes you want to come home, at any second, call me to come get you."

"Yes, Daddy."

"Are your school things ready to go?"

"Yes, Daddy."

"Then let's go. I'll call Mrs Vaughn with the new plan while we're on the way."

8:00 a.m.

"How did Constance like the volleyball match?" Cal asked Michael Renfroe.

"On the way there, she said it didn't sound like something she would pick out to do, but when we left, she said it was fun to watch. She enjoyed meeting Jeri, too."

"Yeah, I picked up on the Jeri thing. I'm not one for needlework, so Jeri was tickled to have someone to talk to."

"Who wound up winning the women's bracket?" Renfroe asked.

"That was a team from Norcross. They were wearing black muscle shirts over black suits. What did you think of the matches?"

"To my unpracticed eye, it was more fun than watching curling in the winter Olympics."

Cal wadded a sheet of paper and threw it at him, hard.

She walked over to his desk and quietly asked, "So, uh ... when are you going to make an honest woman of her?"

Renfroe sat back, gobsmacked for two full minutes, staring into the void.

Eventually, Cal said, "Sorry, didn't mean to interfere. It's just obvious you two adore each other. Seems like a natural progression."

Renfroe blinked a few times and said, "I ... hadn't ... I hadn't thought about that."

Cal rolled her eyes. "I swear, men never do. But you should. Think about it, I mean."

She returned to her desk and said, "Come over when you're ready to talk cases."

Renfroe nodded and quickly reviewed his summary notes, then got some water from the cooler and sat down across from her in Mason's chair.

Which he immediately got up from, because Mason walked in, so Renfroe sat in Mason's guest chair. Being the senior detective had its own (rather spare) perks.

"So," Mason said. He grumbled, "Summarize."

Cal said, "Assuming we have one murderer, we have three suspects that I see. But none of them are perfect."

"Enumerate," Mason said.

"First," Cal said, "Ed Penfield. All kinds of opportunity on the Sauer case, but weak motive. No opportunity on the Argyros case."

"Next," Renfroe said, "Patricia Stancill. All kinds of motive on the Sauer case, but no opportunity. All kinds of opportunity on the Argyros case, but weak motive."

Mason said, "And another thirty or so people had the same opportunity she had on Lilia. Okay, third?"

"Third is Walter Stancill," Cal said. "If he's not telling the truth about wanting to marry Marlene Sauer, he may have decided to get rid of her. Especially if she was likely to turn into another Patty."

"And for Argyros?"

"He felt threatened by her maybe?" Cal said. "Something we could find by digging deep enough."

"And they were involved for a while," Mason said. "But he had no opportunity for either murder. We'll put him on the back burner for now. And somebody *please* figure out why *anyone* would kill Lilia. There is neither rhyme nor reason."

"That we can see," Renfroe said.

"So here's what we do," Mason said. "We lay out the case against Ed Penfield for the Sauer killing to a prosecutor. Let them decide whether to go to the grand jury."

"And Argyros?" Cal asked.

"We tell them what we think might have happened. They

tell us to dig deeper into her life to find any kind of motive. That's where we are right now. Go."

9:03 a.m.

State Attorney (called an Assistant District Attorney in some cities) Cora Heaton was of stout build (but not fat), of gray hair (but not white), of short temper (but not usually angry). She heard the case against Ed Penfield.

"What do you have for physical evidence?" she asked.

"We have a lot of material from the scene," Mason said, "but nothing physical that links him to the crime. No syringe, no bottle of this disinfectant."

"You checked his hotel room?"

"When he was still in it, yes. We had his trash sequestered by the maids. Nothing. And we had all the bottles of disinfectant in the medical building and in their trash checked for prints."

"Thorough," Heaton said.

"We try. Once we found out what to look for, specifically, I mean, we made it our business to look for that."

"If he's not in a hotel anymore, where is he?"

"He's staying at his brother's house," Cal said.

"So without physical evidence, where do you think this could go?"

"Opportunity are us," Mason said. "If we can find motive, we can probably convince him we have physical evidence and get him to confess."

"So, then, motive?"

"Best potential is money problems. He lives in a small town in Mississippi, hasn't had contact with Marlene except for loading a debit card with his alimony payments."

"And you say he had medical knowledge sufficient for a crime like this."

Cal said, "Yes, ma'am. He was engaged to and may have been involved with Sauer when she would have been studying for her board exams. She had finished nursing school in Illinois, but took the boards in Mississippi."

"Let's talk about what evidence you *do* have," Heaton said.

"Okay," Mason said. "A fire was set in a different part of the building. It was slow to produce heat but made a lot of smoke, so whoever set it did so and left the alarm for someone else to pull. Using that as a distraction, and knowing that Marlene Sauer would be the last person out of her practice, they waited for the alarm, and then attacked her with a syringe of disinfectant, injected into a carotid artery."

"Any idea who set the fire?"

"No, ma'am," Cal said, "no prints or other residue on the scene to indicate."

"And you want to indict on this?" Cora Heaton sounded incredulous.

"No," Mason said. "We want *you* to decide whether to indict. With the indictment, we can push harder, get more warrants, more evidence."

"How much do you like this . . ." she looked at her notes ". . . this Edward Penfield for this killing?"

"Mixed feelings," Mason said. "It's not a strong case today."

"But he's all we have," Cal said.

"I'll look at it," Heaton said. "The grand jury sits today and tomorrow. If we decide to go with it, I'll give you a call this afternoon to set the time, as near as we can. Make sure you're dressed for it."

As they walked from the court building back to the police station, Cal asked, "How do I dress?"

"Do you have a two-piece suit and a nice blouse?"

"Skirt or pants?"

"Skirt preferred if it's at least knee-length. Otherwise, pants like you wore to Patty's will be fine. Look conservative. All juries, grand and petit, listen better if you look business-like."

10:10 a.m.

Mason was called to his boss's office.

"I don't like it, Captain. I'm in the middle of two murder investigations, and there's really not time."

Captain Frank Berman looked at Mason with sympathy, but without bending.

"I'm sorry, John. This comes from the chief, and, unofficially, from the mayor. I tried to talk them out of it, but couldn't. A positive mention on NPR leads to more high-income people moving to town, and that means more property taxes."

"It's good to know the mayor has criminal justice as a priority. A low one."

Berman, who had lost fifty pounds but still looked like he had a hundred to go, shook his head.

"Be glad the walls don't have ears. Here are the details." He pushed a sheet of paper across to the detective. "The interview is Wednesday. Be there; do the interview; get back to work."

Mason slapped his palm on the captain's desk, then took

a couple of calming breaths. He snatched the page with the information and walked out without saying anything.

4:30 p.m.

The grand jury heard the case against Ed Penfield around midafternoon. Both Mason and Cal testified as detectives at the scene and as investigators into the death of Marlene Sauer. The jurors returned an indictment for first degree murder after thirty minutes of discussion.

Afterward, Mason and Cal and two officers in a black-and-white drove to the Penfield house and arrested Ed. Ron was just getting home with Young Ed and Lenna in the car; Clarissa was still at work.

"This was inevitable," Ed told Ron. "There's a phone number for a criminal defense attorney I left on the desk. I've already talked with him and told him to be ready. Have him meet us at the jail."

The lawyer, Harley Billings, met Ed at the courthouse, made sure Ed's accommodations would be safe, then went to check on the schedule for arraignment.

Clarissa met Ron at the jail building, where he was waiting to find out what Billings could tell them. While they waited, Clarissa's hands started shaking. Ron clasped her hands to calm her and looked into her eyes.

"What's the matter? Do you need something?"

"No. It's just suddenly ... I'm jonesing for a cigarette."

Ron was surprised. "*Cigarette?*"

"I quit a long time ago, before I married Abe. This is the first longing I've had for one in years."

"Okay . . ."

Ron was trying to figure out something to say when Harley Billings came out of the back hall. Billings was six feet three inches and a fit three hundred pounds, with thinning black hair and a tan, three-piece suit.

"What can you tell us?" Ron asked.

"Ed will be arraigned first thing tomorrow. Arraignment proceedings start around eight, and what time he is heard will be heard depends on the order cases are put in."

"How do you think it will go?" Clarissa asked.

"Several things stack up here," Billings said. "The grand jury's indictment was for first-degree murder. Ed is from out of state, so Cora Heaton will argue he's a flight risk. Chances of bail being set are fifty-fifty; if there is bail, it will be high."

"We can cover it," Ron said quietly.

6:30 p.m.

John returned home Monday night in a foul mood.

Ann wasn't home yet, and Mrs Vaughn said she could stay for another half hour, so Mason put on hospital scrubs and went to the small bedroom he and Ann had set aside for meditation. When he emerged twenty minutes later, his mood had improved from foul to unhappy.

He found Adena in her room working at the small desk he had bought for her early in the fall, after she started staying over on weekends once or twice a month. She was looking at math he recognized as college-level calculus.

He sat on her bed a foot or two from her left elbow and waited.

Eventually, Adena made a final mark on her paper and half turned toward her father.

John said, "I had problems with series equations. I found them hard to visualize."

Adena didn't respond.

"Let's go to the kitchen to say goodbye to Mrs Vaughn, then see what's for dinner."

They both stood and proceeded up the hallway. Adena turned into the restroom, but John continued on to the kitchen.

"How has Adena been this afternoon?"

"You may want to ask her how school was," Mrs Vaughn said, "I could tell you, but it should come from her."

"Okay, thanks for the heads up."

Mrs Vaughn explained how to serve supper, and told him Ann would be late and said not to wait for her.

Just then, Adena entered the kitchen. Mrs Vaughn said goodbye to both of them and went on to her evening.

The table was already set, including hot pads for the large skillet that held the fajita components and the smaller pan that held the warm tortillas. Adena sat in her usual place, and assembled her food carefully, making both assemblages restaurant-perfect.

John watched her as he assembled his own, much sloppier fajitas.

They ate in silence for a few minutes. Then John asked, "How was school today?"

Adena set down her fajita and dabbed her mouth with her napkin. After she swallowed, she said, "Someone helped me today."

"Oh?"

She nodded. "Others were making fun of me, calling me

strange and freak and oddball, but one boy came up and told them to 'lay off' and told them about Mommy dying."

"And did they stop?"

"They stopped. After they left, one came back to apologize. And the boy who told them to stop told me to tell him if they bother me again."

"So," John said. "Who was this mysterious stranger?"

"He was Ed Penfield."

Mason did a double take. Then he remembered. "That's right. The Penfields have a son named Ed. He's named after his uncle. His family used to call him 'Bumper'."

Adena watched her spot. "He was kind to me. No one at school ever helped like that before."

"I'm very glad he did."

Adena resumed eating her fajita.

Tuesday, November 13

9:00 a.m.

The medical examiner released Marlene Sauer's body to Lukas Sauer as next of kin. Lukas had her body transported to Coldiron Crematory, and he arranged for a brief memorial to be held at Pedalino Funeral Home. Contacting the receptionist at the orthopedic practice at Booker Medical Building, he asked that word be spread through the building, and asking that anyone who knew who else he should contact would call him.

When Lukas met Walter Stancill, he immediately he understood why Marlene would be attracted to him. Broad of shoulder and square of jaw, hair of iron gray and eyes to match, a firm handshake — in some these might seem to indicate a fake or "greasy" personality, but in Stancill, they all contributed to his likeability. *And*, Lukas thought, *his shallowness.*

After his peremptory removal from his home, Stancill had attended a couple of social occasions with Marlene on his arm, and she had been well received, so he was able to invite some others to her memorial. Lukas reflected that social norms must be very different for rich Americans.

Lukas knocked on the door of Marlene's neighbors and was assured that they would "be at there."

He also began his inventory of Marlene's possessions. He had no interest in shipping all her goods internationally, so, after a brief phone call with Mason, he decided to donate to charity all that he wasn't keeping. The charity could sell it as thrift or donate it as suited the items and the need.

He also took the time to close out Marlene's apartment lease and her utilities and other accounts, and to have the final bills sent to his home in Leipzig. He contacted her bank and her credit card companies, explaining the situation, and they explained what they would need to conclude her business.

She also had a small private retirement account; he was listed as beneficiary, and the investment firm explained the process of turning her assets over to him. They also explained that he would likely need a US-based accountant who understood the implications of the international transfer.

When printed announcements for Marlene's Wednesday evening memorial went up on bulletin boards at the Booker building, Patty Stancill amused herself briefly with the idea of going. But as much as it would distress Walter — that was her primary reason for considering it — she decided that would just be too tacky.

9:00 a.m.

Ed Penfield's arraignment Tuesday morning went just as Harley Billings had told Ron to expect. They were third in line behind a low-level drug dealer and a breaking-and-entering charge. In Ed's case, the prosecutor argued for high bail or no bail because the accused, as a resident of another state, was a flight risk.

Billings agreed about the need for bail, since his client was not guilty and shouldn't spend any more time in jail; but he asked the judge for a much lower bond amount, since, as an officer of the court in another state, well regarded by his community, Edward Penfield understood the process and was a very low flight risk.

The judge listened to both, and split the difference between the prosecutor's highball request and Billings's lowball request. Which was still a lot of money, but since Ron believed his brother, he put up the required portion, which took a call to his broker. Bail was applied at noon, and Ed was out of jail and on his way home with Ron by two o'clock.

2:00 p.m.

Once they were on the way, Ron said, "We've never talked about exactly what happened last Monday. So tell me now."

Ed said, "I left Amory around one a.m., drove through with a bathroom and coffee stop. Then I sat in my car in the parking lot until eight o'clock. I went into the lobby and to the first reception desk, where I asked where Marlene worked. They told me which practice, so I went there and asked for her. When she came out, I asked if I could speak with her in private. She said they had had cancellations, so she had a few minutes. She led me through a labyrinth that a minotaur would get lost in and into an exam room."

"Coffee?" Ron asked, and Ed nodded. "Describe the exam room," Ron said.

"Ordinary exam room: Cabinets and counters, a chair, a stool, and exam table, a rack of brochures, a couple of posters, one of those blood pressure cuff things no ordinary person can pronounce the name of.

"I sat in the chair; Marlene stood. I told her I knew I had messed everything up after Cory died. Asked her to forgive me. I think she was about to speak when the fire alarm rang. She told me to get out — meaning we could talk later.

"I got completely lost trying to find my way out and ran into Marlene again. She pointed out the exit signs, and I felt stupid. The alarm was continuing to ring, and I got disoriented *again* and took too long to get out. But eventually I made it to the waiting area and out the door."

"Was anyone else in the building by this point?"

"I didn't see anyone until I got to the lobby waiting area."

"There were other people there?" They pulled into the drive through at Great Northwest.

"Yeah. Someone came barreling out of another practice ahead of me and I followed her out of the building. And someone came out behind me, I think from the same office, and followed me. I walked to my car and stood by it waiting until someone came on a megaphone and told us not to leave. Police arrived, and eventually everyone went back inside."

"Drink?"

"Dark roast, heavy cream."

Ron pulled up to the order station and placed their orders. On the way around to the window, he said, "Describe the people you saw in the waiting room."

"The woman in front of me was short, petite, trim, seemed fit; had short, blond hair; wore nurses' scrubs. The woman behind me was tall, gorgeous, dressed for business, not for medical exams."

"That was Lilia Argyros. She was the woman who was killed on Friday."

Ron paid and gave Ed his drink, setting his own in the cupholder.

As they pulled away, Ed said, "I don't think I'll go to the doctor there any time soon."

2:00 p.m.

As financial and other records continued to pour in for both Ed Penfield and Marlene Sauer, Cal and Mason had their hands full. Cal occasionally found something she thought was significant, only to have Mason correct her and tell her it was normal unless there was a pattern. Mason noticed that Cal never asked about the same kind of transaction twice.

Financials and phone records continued to be unrevealing. Ed Penfield was a lawyer, so he had clients, some of whom were criminals in a small way: drunk and disorderly, speeding, occasional trespassing, drugs; but most clients were wills, contracts, lawsuits. Because the charge was murder, the court allowed some extra leeway in looking through his legal practice's financial records. Client records beyond billing were still off limits, however.

Ed's residence at the rehab center was confirmed; his twelve-step meeting coordinator (in Tupelo, Mississippi, not Amory) had confirmed that an "Ed" who matched Ed Penfield's description had been coming to the meetings; he gave the name and number of Ed's sponsor, who confirmed Ed's participation.

Marlene Sauer's financials were, if anything, even more boring than Ed's. They had gone through recent transactions before, but now they were looking further back. Alimony from Ed had almost drizzled to an end, and in fact had stopped for a month six months before, corresponding to Ed's time in rehab. Leading up to that time, as Ed sent less and less each month, things got pretty tight for Marlene; during that month, she had started carrying balances on her credit cards. But when Ed resumed payments, and those larger than required, she had, after three months, paid off all her cards, and she had kept them paid off since.

Michael Renfroe did similar examination of Lilia Argyros's records, and he envied how exciting the other two detectives had it. Lilia's life was mind-numbingly mundane.

The three again watched the video evidence together for both murders. For Monday, they saw Ed Penfield arrive and sit in the waiting area in front of the orthopedic practice. Marlene came to the door and took him in. A few others came and went, mostly patients.

When the fire alarm sounded, people poured out of the entrance to the orthopedic practice. Ed Penfield was last out of the practice, and that at least half a minute after the person before him. As he crossed the waiting area, a small, blond woman came out of the general practice office ahead of him, and Lilia Argyros came out of that same door after him. The three were the last to exit the building.

The next action was firefighters entering the building followed after a minute by a pair of paramedics. One of the firefighters went back out; the timestamp corresponded to the announcement that no one was to leave the premises.

They watched all the way through the time when the building was emptied for the day, noting people entering and exiting each practice and the lab, keeping counts of ins and outs, which matched exactly, with the sole exception of Marlene Sauer. So no one had hidden in the building during the alarm and tried to cover an escape in the confusion.

Friday's video evidence was similarly bland: No one in or out except those who should be in and out.

Mason's only comment was, "We're missing something."

5:00 p.m.

At Mason's request, Ed Penfield arrived at the police station at five o'clock accompanied by his lawyer, Harley Billings. Ed and Billings met at the front door before entering.

In the room with the two-way mirror, which Ed and Billings were both expecting, Ed went back over the entire story for Mason and Cal just as he had told it to Ron earlier. Billings had already heard it as well, so his primary function was to listen to what Ed said and what the detectives said and didn't say.

"And you're certain there was no one else in that part of

the building after you saw Marlene?" Mason asked.

"Didn't say that," Ed said. "There are so many rooms and winding hallways that all I can say is that I didn't *see* anyone. Whether someone was *there* or not is a different question."

After lawyer and client had left, Renfroe came around from the control room behind the mirror, and they discussed what Ed had said.

"Everything lines up exactly with the video evidence," Cal said.

"And you had his clothing and car checked, so he didn't hide anything there," Renfroe added.

"Yes and yes," Mason said. "Even with the indictment, My Friend Cora won't go to trial with what we have. Okay, fresh start tomorrow. Go through every bit of paperwork again. Look for things that don't fit."

Cal and Renfroe nodded and left Mason to review everything in his mind.

6:30 p.m.

Every family has traditions, and now it was a Tuesday, and it was time, since Adena was now living with John and Ann, to introduce her to lo mein night.

Mrs Vaughn had been warned, so she hadn't prepare anything for their dinner.

John arrived home and entered Adena's room, since the door was open, and took his place on the bed next to her elbow as she sat at the desk. To his surprise, she turned toward him immediately, not facing him as such, but paying attention to him.

"Hello, Daddy."

"Hello, Adena. How was your day at school?"

"It was a normal day, except that some people who used to ignore me had heard about Mommy and came to say how sorry they were."

"How did that make you feel?" John asked.

"I was glad to have them talk to me. I was glad they wanted to show me they cared. It didn't help me feel better about Mommy."

John nodded. "And how did you respond?"

"I said thank you to everyone who said something, or to a group if there was more than one person."

"And was anyone unkind to you today?"

"No." Adena wasn't being blunt; she just gave the facts as they were.

"Tonight, we are having a meal that is a tradition for Ann and me."

"Mrs Vaughn did not cook."

"That's right. Every week, Ann and I bring home Chinese lo mein to eat. I hope you will like it. Tonight, Ann will be a little later getting home, so she will put in the order for us and pick it up."

"Does this tradition always happen on Tuesday?"

"Not always. We always try for Tuesday, but sometimes, so that we can eat together, we have to change the night."

"Because sometimes one of you has to work late."

John nodded again. "Yes."

John heard the garage door opening, and told Adena, "Ann is home now. Why don't you get ready to eat and come to the kitchen?"

"Okay."

John went on to the kitchen. "Hey, babe. How are you?"

Ann shed her shoes and hung her coat in the coat closet. She turned and smiled, "I finally got the contracts signed for the big sale I told you about. I couldn't believe how tricky it was to get them to the sale."

"If anyone could do it, it's you."

"You flatter me. But it's also true." Big sales always filled Ann with enormous self-confidence. "Dinner's on the table."

"You won't like this," John said.

Ann arched an eyebrow.

"With Adena here, we are going to have to be civilized and not eat out of the carton."

"I suppose we have to," Ann said, feigning dismay. "Does Adena know how to eat with chopsticks?"

"No, Ann," Adena said from the entrance to the kitchen. "Mommy was teaching me sometimes, but I was not good with chopsticks."

"Why don't you try a little bit," John said, "and then after a few tries, switch to using a fork?"

John got drinks while Ann apportioned the noodles and beef into bowls that they usually used for main-course salads. Adena sat at the table in the place that was now hers and waited patiently.

"How many times should I try to use the chopsticks, Daddy?"

The corner of John's mouth flickered, and he said, "I think six would be a perfect number."

Ann asked, "Why six?"

"It's a joke," John said. "In math, a perfect number is equal to the sum of its divisors, excluding itself. So one plus two plus three is six."

"Daddy, will you show me how to do this?"

"Watch Ann and me one at a time. you will see the same thing from two different angles." So first John and then Ann slowly demonstrated the use of chopsticks. Adena watched, and then tried herself. On the fifth try, she managed to get some food to her mouth, but after six, she reverted to her fork.

When they had finished, Adena asked, "Is it more important for lo mein night to be Tuesday or for us to eat together?"

"It's much more important for us to eat together," Ann said. John nodded agreement.

"Then I will try to be flexible."

Wednesday, November 14

7:05 a.m.

At breakfast Wednesday morning, Ron asked Ed, "The woman who followed you out was Lilia Argyros. Who was the woman who was ahead of you?"

"No idea," Ed said around a mouthful of cereal. "She was short and tiny."

"Like, how short?"

"About five feet, two inches. Maybe only five-one."

"How would you describe her build? The other day you said 'fit.' How? Like a body builder? Or a runner, maybe a soccer player?"

"Could be. Or like … If she were a tweener, like a gymnast."

Ron closed his eyes.

"What —" Ed cut himself off when Ron held a 'wait a minute' finger.

After that minute, Ron opened his eyes. "It's important. I don't know why."

"So," Ed asked after a moment, "what's it like being a high school counselor?"

"Lots of telling kids to hew to the straight-and-narrow while they're in class. A few have to check in on court order. Mostly I do guidance counseling. Had to tell a kid who was failing biology that his dream of following in his father's footsteps as a doctor would probably go unfulfilled."

"Poor kid."

"Worse," Ron said. "He's good at math, so he might make it as an engineer."

Ed snorted. "How'd he take it?"

"I think he was relieved. His ambition may have been impressed on him."

"Dad never did that to us," Ed reflected, eyes lost in the middle distance.

"No," Ron said. "I wonder whether he would consider what I'm doing a step down."

"If your family is provided for, I think he'd be fine with it. I'm just . . ." Ed trailed off.

Ron waited.

"I'm just sorry his last memory of me is a barely functioning alcoholic."

"Dad . . . knew . . . that while you were breathing you still had a chance." Ron suppressed a smile. "He may have been more upset that you became a lawyer."

Ed chuckled. "Yeah, when I started law school, he started telling the catfish joke. To everyone. Repeatedly."

Ron stopped suppressing his smile.

Clarissa entered the kitchen from the back stairs. "Good morning!" she said. "Why the smiles?"

"You mean besides seeing you this morning," Ed asked.

"We were just remembering Dad," Ron said.

Clarissa's face clouded a little. "It's good to have good memories of your father." Ron knew the unspoken end of the sentence was, *I wish I had some.*

9:00 a.m.

Despite his protests, Mason appeared on time at the radio station. He had been ordered by Captain Berman to appear for an interview about cases he had worked that had achieved some wire service attention.

He was being briefed by Darryl, an engineer for the local NPR station.

"This is how it goes," Darryl said. "You'll be on video and audio with the host in Washington, who'll ask questions. If you need to stop and start again, just say, 'Let me start that again.' Leave us a couple of seconds to make editing easier and go again."

"So we aren't live?"

"No, they're recording this, and the crew in Washington will edit it for broadcast. If it's long enough, they'll split it into multiple segments."

Mason was relieved that he wouldn't be on live radio.

The interviewer introduced himself over the video and repeated the instructions to Mason, who figured it couldn't hurt. Then recording started.

"I'm speaking with John Mason, who is a police detective in the Atlanta suburb of Bristow. Detective Mason has been involved in some cases that have had unusual elements, and in at least one case, national implications. John Mason, welcome."

"Thanks," Mason said. "I'm glad to be here," he lied.

"As I said in the introduction, we would like to talk about some of the cases you have been involved with. The first is the death of Barbara Penfield. I understand there was some controversy because of the age of the person convicted of killing her."

"There was controversy, but no question about the facts in the case. Victoria Winstead was an adult when she cut the brake lines on the Penfield car. Her conviction was for a lesser degree of murder because it was impossible, and in my opinion unlikely, that she was targeting Mrs Penfield specifically."

"Who then was her target?"

"It was Barbara Penfield's husband, Ronald. He was the school counselor that Ms Winstead had fallen in love with. When he rebuffed her advances, she decided on revenge. Barbara was taking medication that impaired her ability to drive. We'll never be certain what induced her to drive the car that day, though a phone call was placed to her at home from her husband's school just before she drove away from the house and in the direction of the school; her car's brakes had been sabotaged, and she was unable to stop. Her car ran under a flatbed trailer, causing her death."

"How were you put onto Ms Winstead as a suspect?"

Mason knew he had to fudge his next answer slightly. "By chance I met another student from her school, who told me that when he was working on an older car he had just bought, he had showed her — Victoria Winstead — in general terms how the hydraulic brakes worked. And the car Barbara Penfield was driving was the same make and model, though several years newer."

The interviewer (probably) didn't recognize the pun when

he said, "Shifting gears now, I also wanted to ask you about how you became involved in the death of Senator Charles Jamison. He was a powerful senator, but he died half a world away. How did that come to your attention in Bristow?"

"It started with a local missing person case. A teenager, the son of one of my wife's employees, went missing." Mason did not mention that the teenager, Sean McCloskey, was also the one who had explained car brakes to Vicky Winstead. "Bristow is a tiny suburb, so we have a small police department. Every detective is assigned more than one kind of case all the time. When this teenager was found, it turned out he had been in hiding because he had learned that the senator's airplane crash was not an accident. Sean feared for his safety." Mason didn't mention that Sean had been hidden by Barbara Penfield's husband or that the pilot's widow was the new Mrs Ron Penfield.

"How was Senator Jamison killed?"

"I'm sure you've reported on this. Senator Jamison was in an airplane landing in a fogged-in mountain valley in Afghanistan, and a soldier who had a personal grudge against him rolled the radio landing beacon a couple of hundred feet down a slope, so the small cargo plane made a hole in the mountainside."

"What happened as a result?"

"You have certainly reported on this as well. Senator Jamison was corrupt, exchanging influence over government contracts for cash. Some of those cases have been tried in federal court, some have settled, one or two are still pending. For more details about that, you need to talk to the Justice Department."

"Finally, let's talk about the murder of Nathan Bookman.

How was he killed?"

"In the beginning, this was an ordinary case of murder by gunshot. Nathan Bookman was killed in the foyer ..." He had pronounced it *foy-yur*. "Wait, sorry, this is NPR. Let's start that again. ... Nathan Bookman was killed in the foy-yay of his home by a small caliber gunshot wound to the center of his forehead. But the amount of physical evidence was small — too small to be a coincidence. A few days later, Bookman's girlfriend was killed by a similar weapon miles away in Decatur. Finally, my partner, who I knew as Mark Alcalá, was killed identically to Nathan Bookman."

"Why do you say 'who you knew' as Mark Alcalá?"

"Because it turns out he was actually an agent for a foreign government, Belarus. He was part of a team that was in the area to get hold of some classified material that would give his country an advantage in case it took an aggressive posture against the U.S. or our allies."

"How was Nathan Bookman involved?"

"He was the mathematician who created the classified material. More than that, you would have to extract from the Department of Defense."

"And who was the killer?"

"The killer of all three was Henery Guyée, who had been a janitor at the defense contractor Bookman worked at when he created the classified material. He was also an agent for Belarus and was in fact coordinating the search for the material."

"How was he caught?"

"I had worked at the same defense contractor as both Guyée and Bookman, Kaiser Transceivers, before it went out of business. The material Bookman created, along with everything else from Kaiser and other defense contractors, was stored in a secure warehouse that was protected but otherwise forgotten after nine-eleven. There were higher priorities. FBI agents were already looking into Nathan Bookman, and when he was killed, they joined our murder investigation. I was hosting an Independence Day barbeque for about fifty people at my home, and Guyée was among the attendees. When someone noticed that he feigned illness when he heard the FBI agents would be coming, everything clicked into place, and he was arrested."

"Detective John Mason, thanks very much for speaking to us."

"It has been my pleasure."

The engineer cut the connection to Washington and looked at Mason.

" 'Foy-yur ... This is NPR ... Foy-yay.' Were you making fun of us?"

"Yes, I was."

"Good."

11:15 a.m.

"How was the radio thing?" Cal asked as Mason entered the squad room.

"Fine."

"What cases did they want to discuss?"

"Barbara Penfield, the senator, Nathan Bookman."

"What did you tell them about Bookman?"

"Just the facts."

Renfroe came over. "Did you tell them that Ron Penfield was involved in all those cases?"

Mason's face hardened. "No, I did not. And if anyone asks, *you* won't either."

Both younger detectives were taken aback by Mason's emphasis.

"I'm going to get coffee," Mason said. "When I get back, I need to know what you've learned this morning." He stalked off toward the break room.

The coffee in the pot wasn't enough to fill a cup, so he made more and waited. On his return, Mason said, "Bring what you need to the conference room," and tramped off in that direction.

They complied, Cal finishing a few seconds before Renfroe and waiting for him so they could enter the conference room together.

When they did so, Mason apologized, and with effort calmed himself. "Okay," he said, "Physical evidence. Cal, you first."

"Material from the burning trash can. Just a lab coat with lighter fluid."

"Lighter fluid comes in a can," Renfroe said. "Did anyone find a can?"

"Yes," Cal said. "It was in the trash can with the coat. No prints. Standard Ronsonol lighter fluid, nothing special."

"Any smokers among your suspects?"

"Ed Penfield doesn't smoke. Neither does either Stancill."

"You're calling them *both* suspects?" Renfroe said. "No opportunity. No evidence — and we have the video — that either one entered the orthopedic practice."

"Simply grasping at motive straws," Cal said.

"Enough," Mason said, stopping their evaluations. "Toxicology?"

"Injected in the inner carotid artery using a syringe that had a quarter inch needle and containing a disinfectant. There was slight bruising in a circle around the injection site, and we know what size needle. The poison went directly to her brain. Paramedics on the scene, perhaps five minutes later, saw her convulse briefly and die."

"A deadly substance," Renfroe said, "injected with precision. That would require anatomical or physiological knowledge, I forget which. Which brings us to Patricia Stancill again, with Ed Penfield in second place."

"Opportunity," Cal said.

"You left out something," Mason said, "back in physical evidence. The unknown fibrous bit, and I found another piece of it when I went back to the scene."

"Is that really important?" Cal asked.

"Everything we don't understand is important. Remember that." Mason sat and shook his head. Finally, he said, "Okay, Michael, physical evidence for Lilia. Go."

"Follow the timeline here. Dry grounds in the trash can outside the storage closet where Lilia Argyros kept her espresso machine. Presumably taken out after she had prepped the machine, but before that staff meeting, but she didn't have time to make the coffee because the meeting needed to start."

"She valued promptness," Mason said, "especially where others' time was involved. Go on."

"So before or during the meeting, someone replaces a small amount of coffee with arsenic. Then after the meeting, she's off to the espresso machine, makes her mug full, dumps the wet grounds containing arsenic in the same trash can. She takes her coffee and drinks it at her desk as she's working. Forty or so minutes later, symptoms set in, and she hits the restroom with diarrhea and vomiting. Calls for help. The doctor recognizes the symptoms and injects her with the antidote, but it's too late."

"How many assumptions are in there?" Mason asked.

"The timing is only precise for the start of the meeting and then starting when she rushed to the restroom. The rest is derived from the physical evidence."

"Opportunity?"

"About twenty people."

"Including Patricia Stancill," Cal said.

"What's in her financials? Patricia, I mean."

"Rich people stuff. Her husband left, not by his choice, and moved in with Marlene Sauer," Cal said.

"And before that," Renfroe added, "he was sort-of engaged to Lilia Argyros."

"Okay," Mason said, "get some lunch. Then come back and hit Patty Stancill's background hard. Michael, divide it up evenly, you know how it works. I may be back late in the afternoon. Otherwise, email me a summary and I'll check it from home, probably around nine o'clock."

5:30 p.m.

Ron was home from work about an hour before Clarissa. When she arrived, he turned from topping a pair of homemade pizzas to embrace and kiss his wife. That went on for half a minute until the upper oven signaled it was up to temperature. He started to release her, but she pulled him back for another kiss.

When that kiss was done and her head rested on his shoulder, he said, "Please, dear, not in front of the children," and cocked his head toward the table, where Ed sat with a fair number of papers strewn before him. He politely ignored them.

They released each other. "How was work?" Ron asked as he put the finishing touches on the pizzas. The lower oven signaled its own readiness for the task ahead.

"Pretty good. We brought in two new operators, so I spent the day getting them oriented, reviewing their training records, and giving them a couple of hours of supervision as they started taking calls."

"How did that go?" he asked as he slid the pizzas into the ovens and set the timer.

"Both handled the calls they got. They didn't have to deal with someone so distraught they couldn't understand them. Hopefully they'll settle in pretty well. One took a call in Spanish and was great. They're both fluent in Spanish, which is a big plus in nine-one-one-ville these days."

Ed said, "I guess you got the calls for the two killings at the medical building. Not you, personally; you were still home last week. But your department."

"The Monday event," Clarissa said, "that makes it sound impersonal but for brevity we say 'event' — Monday the fire alarm went first, then the paramedics called the police directly, so we didn't get that call. The Friday event, yes, my department got the call."

Ron asked, "You said when you were at the doctor's office with Bumper last Thursday, you saw Lilia, right?"

He turned on the oven light to check the progress of the pizzas. When he was satisfied, he turned the light back off, but he remained facing the oven.

"Yes, and I met her. She seemed great. And she was gorgeous."

"Stunning," Ed said. "Breathtaking."

Clarissa said, "When we got there she was talking with the receptioninst, but when she heard who we were, she came out of the office into the waiting area to introduce herself. After I met her, she was talking with the receptionist about how on Monday she had seen someone come out of a restroom that had already been checked."

Ron froze in place, still facing the oven. He turned very slowly, facing his wife, looking into her eyes. "Very carefully," he said, "not leaving out anything, anything at all — *not the smallest detail.* What happened after she said that?"

Clarissa's eyes had widened, but now they narrowed as she thought. "The receptionist, Cheree, started typing on her computer. At the same time the door opened, and a nurse called Bumper back to be examined. We got up and went."

"The nurse. Describe her."

"She was very short, just over five feet, I'd say. Blond hair, trim."

Ed was startled. "That sounds just like —"

"Stop!" Ron cut him off. He pulled his cell phone from his pocket entered a number from his contacts. "John," he said, "we need to meet. You need to know what I just learned. ... One hour, Great Northwest. See you then."

He rang off and turned to his wife and his brother. "Listen: Don't talk about anything at the doctor's office together. I need your memories to be unpolluted by each others' recollections."

Both nodded, silent and stunned.

7:30 p.m.

John sat on Adena's bed as she worked at her desk. This time, there wasn't time to wait for her attention.

"Adena, sweetheart."

She shivered. John couldn't tell whether it was from surprise or anger. But she turned to John and looked at the edge of the bed.

"Yes, Daddy?"

"We have to break routine tonight. Mrs Vaughn has left for the evening, and Ann won't be home until late. But I have to go meet someone on police business, and it can't wait until tomorrow. So you have to go with me."

Adena absorbed this for a moment. "What time do we need to leave?"

"We should leave about thirty minutes from now. We are going to the Great Northwest Coffee place. Have you been there?"

"Yes. Mommy said it was the only place she knew where she could get proper Greek coffee. She hated to order it because they called it Turkish coffee."

John grinned. That was Lilia, all right. "Was there something you ordered there? I'll be happy to get it for you if you want."

Adena sat silently.

"But you don't have to decide now; any time while we are there will be fine. Take anything you want to read or work on. We may be there as long as a couple of hours."

"Twenty-seven minutes from now," she said.

8:15 p.m.

At the Great Northwest Coffee Emporium and Meeting Room, Ron bought black coffee for himself and, to his surprise, a Turkish coffee for Mason. Adena asked for a milkshake-like substance, which Mason bought for her.

They settled into a now-familiar corner, while Adena sat at a table nearby with a book.

"Okay, Ron, what is this about?"

"This is about two murders. The two you are working on."

Mason sat up a little straighter. "Okay, but please talk quietly. I have to be careful about what Adena hears, especially about Lilia."

"Understand. I know you can't tell me anything about the evidence. Even if you decided to bend department policy like you did for Barbara, I'm attached by blood to one of the suspects."

"Took the words," Mason said.

"Okay, here's the deal. Are you interested in a person who's a short, petite female? A little over five feet, blond hair?"

Mason didn't reply but the surprise on his face said yes.

"Is she involved in some kind of dance, or maybe gymnastics?"

Mason's surprise was growing.

"Last Monday, she was the third person from the last leaving the building. Ed was next to last, and he saw her. And Lilia was last. Good so far?"

"I can confirm that they were the last three people to leave, but not any hint of our interest."

Ron nodded and sipped his drink. "On Thursday, this tiny

nurse overheard Lilia say that she had seen or heard someone leave a restroom that had already been checked. Lilia was having the receptionist organize a meeting of the entire staff the next morning, Friday, the day she was killed."

"How do you know this?"

"Because Clarissa was taking Ed to the doctor, and she could overhear Lilia talking to the receptionist about setting up the staff meeting. Just as she was saying that, this particular nurse came out to take Bumper back to see someone."

John pursed his lips, lowered his eyebrows. "That shows a possible motive for killing Lilia, assuming this nurse killed Marlene Sauer. But Sauer was killed in the opposite corner of the building. The video evidence shows no one crossing the waiting area and going *into* the orthopedic practice where Sauer worked. And Nurse Petite, we'll call her, came out of the general practice, confirmed by the same video. She *still* can't have killed Marlene Sauer."

"Unless she took a route not seen by cameras."

"There are no communicating doors between practices." Mason was gesturing vehemently.

"She was small and fit and coordinated. A dancer or gymnast."

Mason's voice was clipped and rising, in frustration. "What are you *getting* at?"

"What kind of ceilings do they have?"

Thursday, November 15

8:00 a.m.

Thursday morning first thing, Mason called Clarissa's supervisor to request her presence at the police station. Since Clarissa wasn't on call duty, there was no problem releasing her for the morning.

When she arrived, she was shown to the conference room; Mason was watching the camera view from the control room, just as he had for Walter Stancill's interview.

Renfroe led off. "Can you tell us about what you saw and heard last Thursday?"

"It was mid-afternoon. I had picked up Ed — that's Ron's son and my stepson — at school an hour early. We had gotten a call from the school nurse saying he was complaining about pain in his ears and a sore throat. Ron had called the doctor's office, and they told us Ed could come in if we got there before three o'clock.

"We checked in at the front desk of the general practice. There are several medical practices in the building. Ms Argyros, who worked there, was talking to the receptionist, and when she heard the name 'Penfield,' she came into the waiting area to introduce herself. She had known Ron when she was married to a coworker of his."

Mason both snorted and winced at this. Clarissa was completely accurate, and his own identity did not matter, so she hadn't mentioned it.

Clarissa continued.

"Ed and I sat down. He was immersed in a paperback, and I just waited and observed. Ms Argyros spoke with the receptionist and told her to notify everyone of a staff meeting for the entire practice the next morning at seven forty-five."

Cal asked, "You're certain of the time she called the meeting?"

"Yes. I noticed the posted hours of operation, and on Friday, they see patients starting at eight o'clock, so it connected and made sense. Everyone would only have to be a few minutes earlier than normal."

Renfroe asked, "Did she mention the purpose of the staff meeting?"

"Yes," Clarissa said. "Apparently, when the killing of ... Ms Sauer, was that the name?"

Cal nodded.

"When Ms Sauer was killed on Monday, someone had violated the evacuation protocol, and a clearance notification was hung on the door of a room that wasn't yet empty."

"Wasn't empty?" Cal asked.

"More exactly, someone had come out of a door that had a tag hung on the knob."

The detectives thanked Clarissa and escorted her back to the door.

After she left, Cal returned to the Booker Medical Building to retrieve the video surveillance of the waiting area from Thursday.

Together, the three detectives gathered at Mason's desk to review the footage ("Is it 'footage' if there is no film or videotape involved?" Cal asked) and confirmed that Patty Stancill was the nurse that retrieved Bumper and Clarissa from the waiting area.

When Renfroe and Cal returned to their own desks, Mason rewound the video to the last clear view of Lilia. He stared at it for five full minutes.

9:05 a.m.

Next, the three detectives trudged down the stairs to the forensics lab and asked to see the Sauer evidence. A technician set up the evidence examination room for them, and they went over everything. When they looked at the two unidentified fibrous masses, each about the size of a thumbnail, Mason said, "Hold on to those," and went to the box that contained the white ceiling tiles from the room the fire had been started in.

"It's the wrong color," Cal said.

"These things are sort of yellowish," Renfroe said.

Mason turned a tile over from the white front, which was scorched black over about half its surface, and found a place where the back was untouched by smoke. The two pieces were from that kind of material.

Indicating the pieces, one held by Cal, the other by Renfroe,

Mason said, "We didn't understand these because when you look at the tiles from below, they're white."

They went back to Mason's desk and reviewed the Monday video records. Now knowing what to look for, they found it. Shortly before the alarm, Patty Stancill had carried a box about a foot square and eighteen inches tall into the lab section of the building; a minute later, she had returned to the general practice office in a hurry with the same parcel.

The next stop for the detectives was at the end of a trudge to Cora Heaton's office, where the entire case was laid out for the prosecutor.

"What now?" Heaton asked.

Mason said, "We need your support for a court order to shut down the building, and all personnel to remain there, so we can search the ceiling space for evidence."

Cal added, "We believe we'll find the syringe used to kill Marlene Sauer there."

Heaton placed a phone call, and the four of them trooped to a judge's chambers.

"We have already arrested someone for this murder," Judge Sherles said. "The grand jury indicted Edward Penfield, and I issued the arrest order. Are you certain this will lead to the right killer?"

"Yes, your Honor," Heaton said.

"Let me see it."

Heaton handed them the order they wanted his signature on. He read it and asked, "You won't get hold of anyone's medical records."

"No, your Honor," Mason said.

"It wasn't a question, Detective," the Judge Sherles said, signing. "And the second order?"

"It's for our suspect to open her locker so we can examine the contents."

"Why didn't you look at all the lockers the first time you were there?"

"Because it's in a different part of the building from either the fire or the murder of Marlene Sauer. We're hoping to find evidence there for this one and for the killing of Lilia Argyros."

"Ms Argyros was your ex-wife, yes?"

"Yes, sir. Detective Renfroe has been investigating Lilia's murder. We have reason to believe Ms Stancill committed both of them."

Judge Sherles signed the second order, and they were on their way.

9:30 a.m.

The police descended on Booker Medical Building en masse. All staff and patients were extracted from the practices and the lab, and everyone was told to sit in the central waiting area.

Mr Stotts, the building manager, protested strenuously, but Mason handed him the court order and said, "Tell it to the judge."

Officers took everyone's name and contact information. When that was complete, an officer was dispatched into the crowd to fetch Patricia Stancill. She was brought to Michael Renfroe.

"We haven't met before," Renfroe said, and introduced himself. He handed her the warrant. "This is a court order requiring you to surrender to us all of your personal effects that are on the premises, including opening your locker, your purse and any other items belonging to you, and submitting to a search of your automobile and your person. The last will be accomplished in private by two female officers." He went on to advise her of her Miranda rights.

"My locker combination is sixteen, forty-nine, fifty-two," Patty said. "All of my personal belongings are in there."

Renfroe dispatched an officer and a CSU tech to her locker.

Meanwhile, Mason, Cal, and CSU lead Lanny Johnson entered the general practice and found the restroom farthest from the entrance. Lanny did a quick scan and told the detectives that it was okay to proceed; he knew they wouldn't find anything in the restroom because it had been cleaned several times since Marlene Sauer's murder.

As solid as she was, Cal was still the smallest of the three. Johnson handed her a portable, clip-on sports camera; it would record her activity but not transmit it; Cal attached it to her shirt. They had brought a small ladder for her to stand on; the idea for Patty Stancill was that she had stood on the sink, but Cal was taller and more muscular and easily weighed half again what Patty did, and there was no call to break anything unnecessarily.

Cal topped the ladder and activated the camera. She pushed up on the ceiling tile above the toilet and by the wall, then climbed up into the space above the ceiling.

As expected, she found that the walls only rose above the suspended ceiling by a foot or so. When she stood up straight on top of the wall, she had about six inches above her head and below the building's real ceiling, *or*, she thought, *the underside of the roof.*

Before proceeding with her search, Cal oriented herself to

find the orthopedic practice in the far corner. She inserted a Bluetooth sport headphones in her ears, the kind with a microphone for making a call, turned them on, and called Mason. As he answered, she put her phone in a jogging case strapped to her arm.

"You got me, John?"

"Five by five," he answered. "Is the camera turned on?"

She checked it and said, "Yes."

"Okay, I'm recording audio on my end. Point the camera down here to capture me or Lanny, then proceed at your own discretion."

Cal complied, then began her trek across the wall tops toward the orthopedic section of the building. Skylights provided illumination that was dim but sufficient to maneuver easily and safely.

Wires suspended the tracks that the ceiling tiles rested in from the roof structure, and Cal had to duck under or step across some of them as she took right angles on the path. Progress was slow, both because she was not accustomed to walking on a path less than a foot wide, and because she was watching both the path and the ceiling tiles around her for evidence.

There were many possible routes across the wall tops to her destination, where an officer stood on a ladder in the room Marlene Sauer's body had been found in. On a hunch Cal took the route that had the smallest amount of interference from ceiling suspension wires. Once she nearly lost her balance and caught a wire to regain it.

Cal described her progress to Mason. "There's a lot of dust up here," she said. I'm seeing shoeprints in the dust."

"Get a closeup of a few of them," Mason said, "I wish we

had a way to lift a couple."

Mason must have been on speaker so Lanny Johnson could hear, because Cal heard Lanny say, "Stop where you are, detective. Give me a minute."

Cal waited, and in a minute Johnson's head bobbed up through the ceiling where Cal had ascended, about fifteen feet away.

"I'm going to toss this to you," he said. "Unroll a little and put it down over a shoeprint or two, then roll it back up and toss it back." He measured the toss with his eyes and landed the roll square in her hands.

Cal unrolled the transparent plastic, which was about a foot wide, and placed it sticky side down on shoeprints, a left and the following right prints, where she had not yet walked. Rerolling it, she tossed it back to Johnson and proceeded along the wall tops. She reached the destination without finding anything significant.

Starting back, Cal took a different route, still going slowly to look for ... "There it is!" she exclaimed. "We've got it, John."

"Explain," Mason said.

"I'm looking at a syringe with a hypodermic needle. The needle is covered by a standard cover. It's about six feet off the path I'm on."

"Can you get to it? Or should we go into the ceiling where it is? Your safety is most important here."

"I can get to it," Cal said. "I just have to back up to a corner and follow another wall over ... Okay, I'm standing beside it; it's about a foot from this wall."

"Get good camera shots of the needle's location, then point the camera at the officer over there and point it back at me."

Cal complied, then got an evidence bag from her pocket, picking the syringe up without touching it. By the time she had descended through the ceiling where the nearby officer had stood, Mason and Johnson were there, waiting for her. Camera still on, she marked and initialed the bag as evidence, then surrendered it to Johnson.

10:45 a.m.

Patricia Stancill's fingerprints were taken and compared to the prints found on the syringe from the ceiling. The match was positive, and Patricia Stancill was arrested.

The examination of her locker and its contents found nothing. But a search warrant executed on her palatial home, with the cooperation of the housekeeper, Idell Hendricks, found a one-pound bottle of silvery white arsenic powder. The bottle had been opened; the only fingerprints were Mrs Stancill's; a small amount appeared to have been removed.

12:30 a.m.

Cora Heaton interviewed Patricia Stancill at the police station. Patricia's lawyer, Jeffrey Hambelton, a leading criminal defense attorney, was present.

"Here's what we have," Heaton said. "We have the murder weapon in the death of Marlene Sauer, with your fingerprints and no one else's. Contents of the syringe are being analyzed, but I'm sure they will be this ..." She thumbed through her papers. "... glutaraldehyde. We have prints of your shoes in the ceiling space of Booker Medical, and they were an exact match, including wear and blemishes, to the shoes you were wearing when we arrested you. We have a bottle of the exact arsenic formulation used to poison Lilia Argyros, leaving her daughter *motherless*." Heaton said this bitterly. "The arsenic container was found in the storage shed that held tools used to tend your peach grove, with your fingerprints and no one else's. An amount was missing consistent with the amount found in the trash can, dumped from Ms Argyros's espresso machine."

"Wait," Hambelton said. "How did you establish 'amount consistent?'"

"By experimenting with the machine and some arsenic. And your fingerprints were the only ones on the bottle."

"So what are you asking for?"

"Admit guilt in both cases; fully account for the facts in both cases; and request the mercy of the court. I'll ask the judge for life without possibility of parole, and you'll try to get a no-parole-before date. If it's less than twenty years, I'll fight it. But if you decide to go to trial, I'll go full-bore death penalty. In Georgia, I'll get it."

"Why aren't you going all the way to start with?" Patty asked.

"Because we don't have eyewitness to either act," Ms Heaton said.

Patty was given a legal pad and pen, and Heaton left them to confer.

"Do we have a chance?" Patty asked.

"No."

"I should start writing. Are we private here?" They were in the interrogation room with the two-way mirror.

"Yes. This is a privileged conversation."

"I only have one regret."

"What's that?"

Patty considered, and rejected, sarcastically defining 're-gret.' "I wish I had killed Walter rather than the women."

"From your description, I don't blame you. Now about this confession: You need to assume they have more evidence than they have told us about. Tell everything, make sure that anything else you mention can be corroborated. Otherwise, they will demand a longer sentence."

Patty started writing. Hambelton looked over her confession and called the detectives back in.

2:30 p.m.

Pending the grand jury's expected indictment of Patricia Stancill on Monday, the judge granted remission of Edward Penfield's bail, and released him from the order to stay in the area.

Friday, November 16

8:00 a.m.

"Are you sure you want this, John?" Captain Berman asked. "You have a great future with our department, or you could move to any large department in the country if you want it."

Mason knew that Berman was right. But he knew also what he had to do.

"Captain, I've been troubled by this decision ever since Lilia was killed. I really don't have any choice. My daughter has to come first, and she requires structure in her schedule. My hours and Ann's are too irregular, and in our careers there's not a way around that. We could afford a full-time nanny for her, but what kind of life would that be? Besides, I can resign and Ann can keep working."

"What will you spend your time doing?"

"I can pick up online consulting work. I was a pretty good engineer before Kaiser went under."

Berman picked up Mason's letter of resignation. "There's never a good time for something like this."

"Maybe not good, Captain, but this is the best time possible: I'm between major cases. Caligari can pick up the minor cases — she's completely capable. Maybe have Renfroe or someone keep watch over her shoulder."

"Okay," Berman said. "I'll give Brian Rusher a call."

"Thanks."

8:40 a.m.

"I wish you could stay," Young Ed said as Ed was packing.

Ed shook his head. "Sorry dude, I can't. But you can call whenever you want. Do me a favor and call in the evening, after, say, six-thirty your time."

"Okay. But tomorrow's Saturday. Why not wait until Sunday?"

Ed snorted. "I wish it were that simple. But I have an arraignment on Monday where I have to convince a client to plead guilty so he can get rehab. I managed to get it put off until then, but it won't stretch any more. Plus, I'm going to have to pay my secretary and my paralegal overtime to work this weekend so we can start getting caught up with the work I haven't been able to do while I'm here.

"Okay." The youngster was dejected, and he didn't understand, but he accepted.

"And you: remember what I told you about cheating yourself."

Young Ed nodded gravely.

Ron came in with a question mark on his forehead, but he didn't ask. He did, however, ask, "So when will we get to see you?"

"Maybe around Christmas. It usually slows down a little. Wait . . . What if I get us tickets for the Egg Bowl?"

"Uhhhh," Ron said. "Sportsball. Where are they playing this year?"

"Starkville."

Clarissa and Lenna came in.

"And where, pray tell, would our seats be?"

"In the maroon and white, of course."

"Get a big screen TV and we'll come over and watch at your house."

"Done. Make your plans, get your vacation lined up."

Ron looked around. "This is one of the smallest rooms in the house, and here we all are, packed into it."

Even Bumper laughed at that.

10:00 a.m.

In the registration office, John Mason and Catherine Caligari were happy — more than that — *delighted* to witness the marriage of Michael Renfroe and Constance Wall.

As they walked half a block from the courthouse to the coffee shop for cheesecake — that would be as much reception as they would have — Constance told Michael, "In my father's day, they might have refused to allow us to marry."

Michael replied, "In my grandfather's day — okay, maybe in his childhood — they would have hung me and sent you to live with maiden aunts."

Walking with Cal behind the newlyweds, Mason asked, "So do you two have any kind of honeymoon planned?"

"We both got Monday and Tuesday off," Constance said, "so

we were going to drive up to Louisville to watch horse races and tour distilleries."

"Sounds like fun," Cal said.

Michael asked, "How about you, John. You've resigned — when is that effective?"

"Immediately," John said. "Witnessing your wedding was my last official act as a Bristow policeman."

Constance had not heard about this. "Why are you resigning?"

"I have to help my daughter adjust to life without her mother."

10:45 a.m.

Lukas Sauer finished going through Marlene's possessions. He had set aside everything that looked personal. And he asked Walter Stancill to come and go through her things to see whether there were any personal items he wanted to keep.

Walter politely declined. "After all," he said, "we didn't have enough time to build a life together."

Lukas found some pieces of family jewelry that he would take home. He leafed slowly through a photo album, and he found a business card for the law practice of Edward Penfield. There were plenty of minutes left on Lukas's prepaid cell phone, so he dialed the number.

"Ed Penfield. What I can I do for you?"

"Ed, this is Lukas Sauer."

"Lukas, how are you? I wasn't sure when you were headed back to Leipzig."

"I am flying on *Sontag* — Sunday," Lukas said. "But I was

trying to complete my work on Marlene's apartment, and I found a photo album. It contains pictures I believe you would want."

"That's kind of you. I'm still in town, just about to leave my brother's house; can we meet somewhere so I may see them?"

"I have to wait here at the apartment. Movers are coming to take Marlene's furniture and clothes and I have to be here. Can you come here?"

"Sure. Give me the address and I'll be on my way."

Ten or fifteen minutes later, Ed was standing to the side of the door so movers could exit with the pieces of a bed. When the way was clear, he stepped through the door and saw Lukas standing to one side of the dining room chandelier.

They clasped hands.

"I'm sorry we didn't get to talk more at Marlene's memorial," Ed said, "but I know you had many people to greet."

"Certainly, I understand."

"And now that we *can* talk, I would like to tell you why I was in town on the day ..."

Lukas waited a moment and then nodded.

"Look I know after Cory ... died ... Marlene needed me. She needed a husband, and instead she had a drunk. And she did the right thing by leaving me. She was great, and I was stupid. What I came to town for that day was ... to ... acknowledge how stupid I was, and to ask her to forgive me."

They waited while movers came back through and got smaller pieces of furniture to take to their truck.

"And now," Ed continued, "she's gone. I know I hurt her badly; I hurt your sister. It hardened her for a long time, I think. She may have found happiness with this Walter, but ..."

When Ed paused for a moment, lost for words, Lukas said, "I have met Walter. He might have been good for her for a little while, but . . . " he shook his head ". . . it would not last."

"She deserved better. For all the pain I caused her, for abandoning her for a bottle of liquor, will you forgive me?"

Lukas was startled. But he said, "I forgive you, Ed."

They clasped hands for a moment, until one of the movers interrupted. "Is there anything else?"

"Let me check," Lukas said. He released Ed's hand and went to check behind the movers.

All the furniture was gone; the clothes were gone; the bathroom supplies, the food, the dishes, the cleaning supplies no one from Germany would be without — all was gone.

The only thing left was on the kitchen counter. It was the photo album Lukas had mentioned on the phone.

"No, that is all," Lukas told the mover.

The mover made a notation on some paperwork, then handed the clipboard to Lukas for his signature. He thanked Lukas and mumbled some words of sympathy, and then left, leaving the apartment door open.

Lukas followed him out, closing the door so Ed could examine the photos alone.

Hands trembling, Ed opened the album.

On the first page was a photo from his wedding to Marlene. Marlene and Ed were in the center, with Marlene's parents and Lukas on her side, and Ed's parents and Ron and Barbara on the other side.

The next page held four photos of Ed and Marlene when they had honeymooned in Berlin, and their visit to Neuschwanstein Castle in Bavaria, and the hike to that big waterfall in Switzerland and lifting glasses of lager in Bern.

Tears began to form in Ed's eyes.

After that was a page from the time Marlene had been pregnant, four views of her size increasing from picture to picture.

Tears now streamed freely down Ed's face, each hanging onto his chin until nudged off by the next.

Next there were pages and pages of Cory: as a newborn, an infant, a toddler.

Ed couldn't help himself, looking and turning pages, laughing and sobbing all at once. Mercifully, there were no pictures of Cory when he was obviously ill or hospitalized.

But the last two pages destroyed Ed completely. He sat on the kitchen floor and bawled and wrapped his arms around his knees, sobbing until he had no breath left. The next to last page was a full-page picture of Cory's tombstone. The final page was Marlene's copy of their divorce decree.

When Ed had quieted, Lukas opened the door, pausing to make sure Ed was really done. He told Ed, "I'm glad you came."

They embraced and said goodbye, and Ed got on the road to Amory.

11:16 a.m.

Walter Stancill was met at his front door, backpack in hand, suitcases left in the car, by Idell Hendricks.

"It appears Patty won't be coming home," he said.

"No, sir."

"I'm going to need your help arranging for all her things to be sold."

Idell waited.

"No one knows Patty or Patty's things like you do. I need help separating what she would want to keep from what will be outdated."

"In twenty-five years minimum."

"Mm-hm."

"This requires a level of expertise that I am not currently being paid for."

"Direct," Stancill said. "I like that."

"On *this* subject you like it. Be careful what you ask me about. About pay ..."

"Double what you make now."

Idell considered. That brought her to three times the average for a chief housekeeper in Arcadia Commons — even more than the Vega's head housekeeper.

"All right. Three months minimum, five eight-hour days per week. Plus, my normal duties. And I'll need to hire one additional staff, full-time, live-in. We have room available in the staff quarters. And ..."

"... yes ...?"

"No 'extracurricular activities' with *any* of the staff."

"Agreed."

Stancill entered the house and took his laptop to his room. Idell called for one of the maids to get his suitcases.

Sunday, November 18

10:00 a.m.

For reasons she couldn't quite put her finger on, Ann volunteered to take Adena to church on Sunday. She observed the Greek Orthodox service with interest and was surprised at the clarity of what was said and sung and chanted and recited.

As they left the Divine Liturgy, an assistant priest introduced himself and said hello to Adena. He asked Ann how they were related.

"I'm married to Adena's father."

He nodded and said to Adena, "We were all so sorry to hear about your mother."

"Thank you," Adena stared at a corner of the sidewalk behind him.

"I saw you here last week with a gentleman. Was that your father?"

"Yes, sir."

To Ann he said, "Did one of you have an Orthodox background?"

Ann shook her head. "No, neither of us had much of a religious background."

"I understand," he said. "My presbytera — sorry, my wife — also had no religious background."

"Wait," Ann said. "You can marry? I thought . . . "

He chuckled. "A common misunderstanding. Orthodox priests can marry before ordination. My wife and I frequently have guests for an early afternoon meal on Sunday. We would be delighted if you could join us."

Ann's mind raced. "That's very kind of you, but we need to be getting home."

He smiled and nodded. "I understand," he said. "But the invitation is open any Sunday when we are here."

"Thank you."

Adena said, "Thank you, Father."

Monday, November 19

8:00 a.m.

First thing on the Monday following, the grand jury rescinded its indictment of Ed Penfield. It also indicted Patricia Stancill for two murders.

That afternoon, Judge Sherles accepted Patricia Stancill's confession and the plea agreement, and he heard sentencing arguments. He had warned attorneys to be ready. Cora Heaton, the prosecutor, asked for life without possibility of parole; defense asked for twenty years before eligibility for release. The ruling was life in prison, parole-eligible in thirty-five years.

Tuesday, November 20

8:47 a.m.

Mason's radio interview was broadcast in two parts on consecutive days, interspersed with repeated audio of the broadcasts related to the Jamison case. After the second part ended on Tuesday, the radio host added this epilogue:

"That was part two of our interview with John Mason, a police detective in the Atlanta suburb of Bristow. As an update, since we recorded the interview last week, Detective Mason has resigned his position with the Bristow police. He and the Bristow police confirmed his resignation, both saying only that the reasons were deeply personal."

www.ingramcontent.com/pod-product-compliance
Lightning Source LLC
LaVergne TN
LVHW100527110826
845146LV00002B/801

* 9 7 9 8 9 9 9 2 5 9 5 3 0 *